"Who is this?" I pleaded. "At least give me a hint."

"Okay," the voice said. "I gave you something of mine. Tonight."

"Tonight?" The only person I had seen that night was . . . "Is this Sandra?"

"My friends call me Sandy."

"Uh, okay." Why didn't she just say Parker the Pig?

"I forgot something tonight. My eye shadow. It was in the bottom of the bag I gave you."

"Oh."

"Well, if it's still there, why don't you give it to me at school on Tuesday? I don't think I'll need it before then." She sighed. "Not unless I have a date or something."

If I hadn't known better, I would've thought she wanted me to ask her out.

FROG EYES
LOVES PIG

By James Deem

CROSSWINDS

New York • Toronto
Sydney • Auckland
Manila

For Susan

First publication August 1988

ISBN 0-373-98030-2

RL 4.7, IL age 12 and up

JAMES M. DEEM earned his M.A. and Ph.D. degrees at the University of Michigan, where he won the Hopwood Award for fiction in 1975. Currently assistant professor and director of the communications skills program at John Jay College of Criminal Justice, he lives in Westchester County, New York, with his wife and twin daughters. He is also the author of *How to Find a Ghost* (Houghton Mifflin).

Chapter One

It may have been my sixteenth birthday, that first Friday in September, but I was in no mood to celebrate. Especially when I asked my parents if I could use one of our cars and they told me to use my little brother's bicycle instead.

"I'll be right back," I said. "I just want to buy some shampoo."

"You'll burn two gallons of gas," the Duke (my father) replied. I thought of him as the reincarnation of John Wayne. He was tall, silent, and stubborn—plus a little bowlegged.

"But this could be another birthday present," I continued in my most diplomatic tone.

"I think you did pretty well for your birthday already," the Duke reminded me.

"You're right," I agreed. Contact lenses and my driver's license weren't bad presents, even if I had asked for an Apple computer. They had even given me the contacts a month early, just so I'd be able to break them in before school started. But, then, I really needed them, now that I had been appointed feature editor of the Ocotillo High School newspaper.

Throughout high school, I had been the skinny kid with half-inch-thick glasses who worked on the school newspaper. Actually, I had worn glasses since the third grade, but I had gotten noticeably thinner and taller, not to mention more awkward, in high school. My eyes had also gotten much worse, so much so that some kids called me Frog Eyes. I could hardly blame them. My glasses were so thick I could fry ants on the sidewalk with them.

But that fall I had formulated a self-improvement plan. Being feature editor was a good start, since it was one of the most important jobs on the paper. But I wanted to be known as the good-looking feature editor of the *OHS Observer*. I also wanted to enhance my popularity. And I knew that handsome, popular feature editors didn't ride their little brothers' bikes to the drugstore.

"What about if I pay for the gas?"

I thought he might give in then, but my mother interrupted. She looked up from the TV where they had been watching the end of the *MacNeil/Lehrer News Hour* and asked, "What kind of shampoo did you want?"

"Why?" I asked suspiciously.

"There's nothing wrong with the shampoo I buy. And there's a new bottle of it in the hall closet."

"But, Mom, that stuff gives me dandruff."

"Oh, that's just your imagination," my mother said. "It's expensive shampoo."

"Mom, it's not my imagination. Does this look like my imagination?" I asked, running my hand back and forth through my hair, watching the dandruff flecks fly.

I could see the headline in tomorrow's paper:

BOY SUFFOCATES PARENTS
WITH DANDRUFF AVALANCHE

"So what do you say?" I inquired again, pleasantly enough considering that I was running out of patience. "Okay?"

The Duke sighed. "Correct me if I'm wrong, but I think I said 'no' once tonight," he told me.

"I don't believe you," I said. "I mean, it's my birthday, and you won't let me use the car. What'd you let me get my license for? I'll be the only kid at school who can't use the car." I knew I was exaggerating a little, but I couldn't stop myself. "You aren't fair."

"Your bike awaits," he added. He was being "cute." That's what happens to kids who have fathers in advertising; their fathers are always acting clever.

"I'm not a child anymore, you know."

The Duke swiveled his head toward me like the rotating cannon on a tank. "Then be an adult and use your brother's bike," he said.

"But I don't want to use Rich's bike."

He decided to ignore my remark. "Allan, if you don't mind, we wanted to watch this program."

Some fish swam by on the TV screen, and I thought, *Great! Some PBS documentary on rare fish in the Aegean Sea is more important than me and my problems! That shows their priorities.*

"But what if someone sees me?"

"Whine-o Alert," my father quipped.

"But I'd die if—"

"Goodbye, Allan. Go harvest your dandruff."

So there I was, sixteen and carless, pedaling my little brother's Stingray to the drugstore. I rode down the street to the start of a dirt road that ran alongside an old irrigation canal, the kind of canal that crisscrossed Phoenix everywhere. The road, which bordered the back of our subdivision, would eventually come out at Cactus Drugs, my home away from home. When I was younger and less proud, I'd ride there to browse the magazine rack or buy a Creamsicle. Now I wouldn't be caught dead going there on the bike, unless I was desperate.

And I was desperate. What I didn't tell my parents was the real reason why I wanted to get to Cactus Drugs so badly. It wasn't for the shampoo, though I did want some. I had decided to buy myself a birthday present as part of my self-improvement plan for junior year, and I had to wait till evening, when the drugstore was less crowded, to buy it.

My self-improvement plan consisted of a number of other steps, besides getting contacts and being feature editor. I wanted to be named Ocotillo's teen correspondent to the *Arizona Register*, the Phoenix morning paper, a position I had applied for in June. Then I wanted to make some new friends and find a beautiful, sexy girlfriend. If I could manage to do that, my plan would be a success. But first I had to buy my birthday present. I needed an education beyond what I was getting in school.

By the time I chained Rich's bike to one of the steel pillars in front of the store, the armpits of my shirt were ringed with sweat. The temperature had been 110 degrees that day and, though the sun was setting, the air still felt like an oven, which was one more reason I had wanted to use the car: at least it had air conditioning. But I had to admit that I would probably still have walked into the store with mile-wide sweat marks, regardless of the weather. As long as I had decided to buy myself this particular present, I was going to be a nervous wreck.

Inside, I quickly surveyed the store: one check-out girl, two people in line, one customer at the prescription counter, the pharmacist, four or five other people wandering around and that was all. I hurried to the shampoo aisle and found the kind I wanted. Then I scanned the deodorants to try to find the one that really stopped wetness; some days I was more fish than human. In my rush I didn't see one that would help.

Finally, I walked determinedly to the magazine rack. There, I began to search for the title I wanted. When I didn't see it, I began to panic. I tried to take a deep breath, and I made myself look again, this time more slowly.

Almost as an afterthought, I happened to look down at the magazines on the bottom shelf, where I noticed a large stack of magazines with the top copy turned down. I flipped the magazine over: *Playboy*. Automatically, I whipped my head around to see if anyone had noticed, but no one was nearby.

I might as well say that I know there is only one purpose for *Playboy*, and it's not the articles—every boy knows that. I was certain that an alarm would go off at any second or that my mother would see me and fall into a dead faint, since I had to be committing a crime by even touching the magazine. But I had decided a few weeks earlier that I was old enough to buy it now. I had seen it at school, passed around the cafeteria for lunchtime reading (if you could get the pages unstuck), and I had gazed at other magazine counters longing for the courage to buy my own copy. Then my little brother Rich had come home with one he had swiped from a friend. The time had come to improve all of me.

I quickly picked up a copy and pressed it against my side. Then I grabbed up the latest copy of *Fangoria* to cover it with.

Two women were ahead of me in line. I carefully laid the magazines on the conveyor belt, with *Fangoria* prominently on top, and set the shampoo nearby. Then I took a deep breath and acted as if I were doing the most natural thing in the world. I already knew what I'd say if someone said I was too young or asked why I was reading trash: I needed it for a story I was writing for my school newspaper on the availability of adult pornography. It was a dirty job, but somebody had to do it. After all, I was feature editor, and that meant exploring all kinds of subjects. I took another deep breath and waited my turn.

"Allan?"

I nearly fainted. I glanced around and saw Sandra Parker (a.k.a. Parker the Pig), who sat next to me in sophomore English. She was wearing a baggy blouse that ballooned over her hips, trying to hide all of her excess baggage. And I was standing there, looking like a plucked chicken, with my arms glued to my sides, trying to hide my sweaty armpits. We made a great pair.

"Oh, hi." I was aiming for nonchalance, but I had already started to panic. How was I going to get out of the store with the *Playboy* undetected?

"How are you? What're you doing?" she asked, edging up behind me.

"Not much, getting some shampoo," I said, nodding to the counter.

"Me, too," she said, sounding thrilled at the coincidence.

I heard the front door swing open, and I looked to see if someone from Ocotillo was walking in. I didn't want to be seen talking to Parker the Pig, especially now that I had contacts.

"Did you get contacts?" she asked suddenly, scrutinizing my eyes.

Without thinking, I started to smile. "Yeah, I got them for my birthday."

"That's really nice," she said, beaming back at me. "When was your birthday?"

"Oh, well, actually, t-today is my birthday," I said, feeling suddenly tongue-tied. "But I got my contacts last month so I'd have a chance to break them in before school started."

"You look really good in them."

It's true: I wanted people to notice the new, handsome me. But "people" didn't include Sandra Parker.

"How did you know I got contacts?" I asked then.

She looked at me as if I were stupid. "Because you're not wearing your glasses, silly."

"Oh, yeah." I smiled dumbly. I had hidden my glasses away in my dresser drawer. I never wanted to wear them in public again.

"How are you tonight?" the cashier interrupted.

"O—" my voice caught; I cleared my throat. "Okay."

She picked up the shampoo and punched its price into the cash register, then she rang up *Fangoria* after glancing at its cover. Next, she turned over the *Playboy* and seemed to take an eternity to find the price.

Then Sandra leaned forward and whispered, "Quite a combination."

I closed my eyes, as if I were about to be executed, and said nothing.

Finally, the cashier totaled my purchases, and I handed her a ten-dollar bill. As I extended my arm, I watched a drop of perspiration fall onto the counter, and I winced. I quickly pocketed my change and grabbed the sack.

"Bye, Allan," Sandra called after me.

"See you Tuesday," I replied, without thinking. Tuesday was the first day of school for the year.

Tuesday? I thought to myself as I stepped on the electronic door mat and the out door flew open. *Why did I say that? I don't want to see her Tuesday or any other day of the year.*

I was almost out the door when I realized that someone was approaching the in door. For some dumb reason, I glanced at the person and immediately wished I hadn't.

Brian Sawyer, one of the biggest no-neck jocks at school, was looking right at me, a big smirk plastered on his face.

Chapter Two

Hey, Frog Eyes! How's it going?" he called loudly.

Couldn't he see that I had contacts now?

"Ribbit," he croaked as I sailed past him. "Ribbit."

As I hurried to Rich's bike, I heard the woosh of the electric door, opening and closing for Brian. Quickly, I unlocked the bike, but in my rush I jammed my foot against the kickstand and managed to sprain my big toe. Next, as I tried to ride away, the bag ripped and the shampoo and magazines fell on the sidewalk. Then Sandra Parker left the store.

It was definitely not my night.

"Did you break your shampoo?" she asked, rushing over to me. I saw that the *Playboy* had opened to a page of posing bunnies, and I grabbed for the magazine.

"No, I just ripped the bag," I told her, aware that my face was flushed. I was also aware that Brian could walk out of the store at any second.

I could already see the headline for what Brian thought:

FROG EYES LOVES PIG

"Here, take mine," she said, removing the shampoo and a few other items from her bag. "You need it more than I do."

"You sure?" I asked.

"Yeah, my car's right there," she said, pointing to her Chevette. She handed me the bag. Quickly, I stuffed everything into the new bag and was ready to say goodbye, when Brian Sawyer reappeared, opening a pack of Marlboros.

"Hey, Froggy, can't get your bike in gear?" he asked, stuffing a cigarette in his mouth. He had stopped a few feet away from his car, but he didn't seem to notice Sandra. He flicked his butane lighter and inhaled. Then, blowing a cloud of smoke toward me, he said in his nastiest voice, "Where's Harry? Bet you can't wait to see him Tuesday." Then he got in his Camaro and left a trail of rubber on his way out of the parking lot.

"What a creep," I said.

"Why'd he say, 'Where's Harry'?" Sandra asked. "Did he mean Harry Snyder?"

"It's a long story," I told her, one that I wasn't going to share with her. "Thanks for the bag," I said and rode away.

At home I was still fuming about Brian as I parked the bike in the garage. Then, to be safe, I extracted the *Playboy* and stuffed it down the front of my pants. Next I pulled out my shirttail and walked into the house. My mother and the Duke were engrossed in their fish show, so I began to steal down the hall to my bedroom.

"Come here a second," the Duke called, stopping me in my tracks.

"Why?" I asked hesitantly. What if they found the *Playboy* after all?

"Just come here," he repeated.

I turned around and walked slowly back down the hall. I stopped at the breakfast bar, where I could keep my distance, and asked, "What?"

"What're you so cranky about?" the Duke asked.

"Nothing."

"You could've fooled me," he said.

"I sprained my toe on Rich's kickstand, and I saw two people I know. And both of them were driving," I told them. "Is that all you want?'' I asked, turning a little too stiffly toward the hall.

''Harry called,'' my mother said. After my encounter with Brian, that was all I needed. ''He wants you to call him.''

''Tonight?''

''I told him you just rode down to Cactus Drugs,'' my mother explained.

''On the bicycle? You told him I rode a bicycle?''

My mother just looked at me like I was crazy.

The Duke got up then and walked toward the kitchen. I started to turn away from him, so he wouldn't see the *Playboy*. He put his hand on my neck and squeezed it lightly.

''Sit down a second,'' he said, pushing me onto a bar stool. I felt the sharp, glossy pages of the magazine digging into my waist. ''You know we're going to let you use the car, don't you?'' He squeezed my neck again.

''Yeah, I know,'' I said.

''You know I put you on the car insurance today. Right?''

I nodded.

''Then give me a break with this bicycle crap. Please? When you need to use the car for something important, you can use the car. You know that. But I wouldn't call going to the drugstore important, no matter how bad you think your dandruff is.''

I shrugged and said, ''Okay.''

''You make us out to be villains when we really aren't,'' he said.

''Don't start with a sermon,'' I said, pulling away from him. ''I just can't help myself sometimes. Mom says I'm just as stubborn as you are.''

He patted my back and laughed. ''Okay,'' he said, as I started to walk away.

''Don't forget to call Harry,'' my mother added.

''Right,'' I muttered.

But the truth of the matter was that I didn't want to call Harry. Not tonight and not ever.

The problem with Harry wasn't Harry himself. I mean, I liked Harry; we had been friends since grade eight. But it was harder to be his friend now. During sophomore year, we were best friends. We were in four classes, so we walked to class and ate lunch together. We went to every football and basketball game together. After he got his driver's license in February, he even drove me home most days. Then in early March, when he found out his parents were getting a divorce, we spent the rest of the school year driving around Phoenix, talking about his parents' fights and the custody agreement. I felt really sorry for him, because I hated to see a friend get messed up.

No, the problem with Harry wasn't Harry. The real problem with Harry was Brian Sawyer. And that was the story I didn't want to tell Sandra Parker.

The whole mess had started during sophomore year in Spanish II, which both Brian and I took. Brian may have been one of the biggest jocks on the football team, but he was the laziest student in Spanish II. On the other hand, I was the only straight-A student in the class, a fact that Mrs. Castillo, our overaged teacher, drilled home daily.

"Thank you, Allan," she'd said, after she volunteered me to give a correct answer when everyone else had failed. "If everyone else studied as hard as you...."

I'd roll my eyes in agony and secretly hope that no one would hold it against me. Of course, Brian hated everything I did and called me Froggy or Frog Eyes or ribbeted at me every chance he got. I'm sure he could tell that my Kermit biceps weren't going to make a dent in his steer hide. Basically, I just ignored him, the way I ignored anyone who decided that my glasses were good for a joke. I managed.

Then one Friday in early April, when we were taking our weekly vocabulary quiz, disaster struck. That Friday I finally got Brian's paper to grade.

At first I was thrilled that Brian missed six of the ten questions. My dilemma was how to mark the *F*. Part of me wanted to plaster a big red *F*, five inches high, across the top of his paper and then write a comment like, "Why don't you study for a change, bozo?" But since I valued my health, I settled for a very small *F*, which I positioned carefully under his name.

"Please pass the paper back to its owner," Mrs. Castillo requested. Papers began to flutter across the room. "Now call off your grade when I read your name." This was Mrs. Castillo at her laziest. She never looked at the quizzes herself. The rumor was that she was just waiting to retire and move to Acapulco.

I was the first to report, as always.

"Allan Antottle?"

"A," I almost whispered. I was happy with the grade, but I didn't like to be the center of attention grade-wise.

She clucked approvingly and marked the grade in her book. While she proceeded alphabetically, I kept a tally of my competition. No A's, eleven B's, five C's, two D's.

"Brian Sawyer?" I heard her ask.

"C," he replied in a confident tone.

"No, that was an—" I corrected, without thinking.

"Is there a problem, Allan?" Mrs. Castillo asked.

"I wrote an *F*," I said, before I realized that it was a mistake to dispute anything that Brian Sawyer said. I added quickly, "I think I wrote it too small. It was hard to read."

"How many questions did you miss, Brian?"

He took his time counting them up. "Six." Then he added, somewhat sheepishly, "I guess that wasn't a *C*."

She was silent a moment, then resumed recording the grades. When she had finished, she said, "I think I'll collect the quizzes today. Please pass them to the front."

When I turned around to take the papers from the girl behind me, Brian looked like he wanted to turn me into Alpo.

After class, I quickly headed for the door. I was so worried about Brian that I didn't even wait to meet Harry, which I always did. I just started walking, and I didn't look back. I was halfway to World History before Brian caught up to me. I knew I had to talk fast.

"I'm sorry I said anything," I apologized. "I should've—"

"It's okay," he said, then shrugged. "I thought it was worth a try. Castillo's a pain anyway."

I couldn't believe he was taking it so well. "Well, I didn't mean to—"

"Where's Harry Snyder?" he interrupted. "Don't you always walk with him?"

I looked at him suspiciously. "Usually," I replied. "I'm just in a hurry today, that's all. I have a story to write."

"That's good," he said. Then he added sarcastically, "For a second, I thought you two had a fight or something. You know, a lovers' quarrel."

I stammered and blushed, but I couldn't find any words to say. Then Brian put his jockey walk into high gear and passed me by.

I figured that my punishment was over, but it wasn't. Almost every day after that for the rest of the school year, whenever he saw me without Harry, Brian asked "Where's Harry?" in a nasal tone of ridicule. His "Where's Harry?" had so much implied scandal that it was useless to fight back; he made us sound so queer that all I could do was glare.

The Duke had a phrase for it. Whenever someone knew how to get him mad without even trying, the Duke said, "He has my number." Well, Brian not only had my number, he called me every chance he got.

Poor Harry never knew what was happening. He just kept driving me around, complaining about his parents' divorce. But junior year was going to be different. I didn't want to be thought of as Harry's clone anymore, mostly because I didn't want Brian Sawyer bugging me about Harry anymore. The only way for that to happen, I was sure, was to find a new best friend.

Chapter Three

I had just put the Cactus Drugs bag on my bed and the *Playboy* under my mattress, making plans to look at my treasure, when my brother Rich walked in.

"What're you doing?" he asked.

"Nothing," I said. "What're you up to?"

"I'm spending the night at Brad's," he said. "Then Coach is taking the team up to Saguaro Lake for the weekend."

"The whole JV football team?" I asked skeptically.

"Yeah, Coach says we need to build some team spirit. Anyway, Brad knows these girls that're going to be camping there."

"Sounds like fun," I sighed.

Rich may have been a year younger than me, but he always had something to do, somewhere to go and someone to give him a ride. I had to admit—but not to him—that he was just more popular than I was.

"Could I use your sleeping bag?" he asked then.

"What's wrong with yours?" I asked, knowing perfectly well what was wrong. Rich still wet the bed sometimes, something that really embarrassed him. At least I was more successful at bladder control, even if it didn't count for anything.

"Nothing," he said, "forget it."

"It's okay," I insisted, feeling a little ratlike. "You can use it."

"Not if you don't want me to."

"Rich, go ahead and use it," I practically begged him. I figured he'd probably tell my parents if I didn't let him have it. But I added, "Just be careful, you know?" He pulled the sleeping bag from my closet shelf. "Want to see something?" I asked, trying to take advantage of my temporary victory. I reached under the mattress and pulled out the *Playboy*. "Look at this."

"That the one with the blonde? She's using the barbells?"

"I don't know, I—" I flipped to the centerfold. "Yeah." I felt foolish for not knowing.

"I saw it already," he said. "Last month's was better."

"Yeah," I said. I wasn't going to tell him I hadn't seen last month's.

I flipped through the *Playboy* absentmindedly, waiting for him to leave.

"You should get the real thing instead. It's a lot more fun," he said.

"What do you know about the real thing?"

"A lot more than you think," he replied. "What're *you* doing tonight?" he asked then. "Got a hot little blond number lined up?"

Then he hurried out of the room with the sleeping bag before I could say anything more. I imagined the perfect headline:

TALENTED TEEN SLAYS BROTHER
ON BIRTHDAY, SHOWS NO REMORSE

I could hear the phone ringing a while later, and I knew it would be Harry. He'd probably wish me a happy birthday and then ask me to come over and watch *Monty Python* or *Star Trek* reruns on his VCR. If I was really lucky, he'd tell me his mother was home, planning to make us a big bowl of buttered

popcorn. We'd be enacting another installment of "The Allan
and Harry Show," a show that I hadn't minded last year. But
I needed a new show and a new cast this year.

"Allan!" my mother yelled on schedule. "It's for you!"

"All right, all right," I muttered and threw the *Playboy* un
der my bed.

"Hello?" I asked a moment later and waited for Harry's
monotone. I was going to try to tell him I had other plans.

"Hi." I heard a cute, female laugh.

"Hi," I replied. But the voice said nothing. "Who is this?"

"You know," the voice teased.

I laughed. "No, I don't."

"Yes, you do," the voice said impatiently, still teasing.

I laughed again, intrigued. "Are you sure you don't have the
wrong number?"

"Not if this is Allan Antottle."

"Who is this?" I pleaded.

"Well, if you don't know, I'm not telling you."

"At least give me a hint."

"Okay," the voice said. "I gave you something of mine."

For some reason, I started to blush. "Wh-When?" I wanted
to know.

The female caller clucked her tongue. "You're no fun," she
said. "Tonight."

"Tonight?" The only person I had seen that night was... .
"Is this Sandra?"

"My friends call me Sandy," she told me.

"Oh, okay," I said. Why didn't she just say it was Parker the
Pig?

"I forgot something tonight."

"What?" I asked suspiciously.

"Unless you can use it." Then she laughed again. The laugh
still sounded cute.

"Use what? What're you talking about?"

"Eye shadow," she said matter-of-factly.

"Eye shadow?"

"I forgot that it was in the bottom."

"What?"

"Of my bag. The one I gave you."

"Oh," I said, finally understanding her.

"Is it there?" she asked.

"I don't know."

"Didn't you unpack it yet?"

"No," I said.

"I thought you would've emptied the bag by now," she teased. "If you know what I mean." I was too embarrassed to say anything. "Well, if it's there, why don't you give it to me at school on Tuesday? I don't think I'll need it before then." She sighed. "Not unless I have a date or something."

If I hadn't known better, I would've thought she wanted me to ask her out.

"Well—"

"Well what?" she asked quickly.

"It's just that I don't know if I'll see you on Tuesday. I mean, we may not have any classes together."

"I'm sure I'll run into you—somewhere. Anyway, I'm working in the office sixth hour. So even if you can't find me, I'll find you sixth hour."

Sixth hour I had journalism. I could just see Sandra Parker waddling into the j-room, in front of the whole staff, asking me for her eye shadow. God, what was everyone going to think?

BOY STALKED BY PIG WEARING EYE SHADOW

I'd have to head her off somehow.

"No, I've got journalism then. I'll probably be working on a story. Why don't I just leave it in the office for you?" I suggested.

"Why would you want to do that?" she asked. "I'll come by and pick it up when I get the attendance slips."

"No, really, I'll just leave it in the office."

"What's the matter? Don't you want me to come into journalism?" she asked.

"No, no, that's not it," I insisted, a little too quickly. "It's just that I might be out on assignment or something."

"I'll track you down," she teased.

I wasn't going to argue; I was just going to leave it in the office anyway. "Okay, well, I'll check the bag and give it to you on Tuesday. If it's there."

"Sorry about all this," she said.

"Goodbye," I said.

Then I went back to my room and picked up the *Playboy*. As my eyes roamed over Miss September's body, I kept hearing Sandra's voice: cute, sexy, taunting. Then I matched her body to Miss September's, and I felt cheated. How could she sound that good and be that fat? Why couldn't she be skinny and cute? Then I wondered, why was I dwelling on Sandra Parker at all?

That was a question worth thinking about, but Miss September took over.

Chapter Four

School started the Tuesday after Labor Day. I had made it a rule, on the first day of junior year, to make one new friend as part of my self-improvement plan, but I didn't see one promising face anywhere during my first two classes.

I moved on to homeroom, hoping to find a better crowd and just one friendly face. But after I had surveyed the group and found no one, I sat there feeling more than a little dejected, listening to the two biggest junior gossips in front of me.

"Who?" one of them was asking after the announcements had been aired.

"Beth," the other answered.

"Matthews?"

"Yeah."

"Really! How long?"

"Three months."

"Who?"

"Some sailor from San Diego."

They laughed.

"And Barry Lunstrum. Did you hear?"

I happened to turn then and notice that the guy sitting next to me was paying as much attention to them as I was. I made a face about the conversation.

"Some people have no class," he agreed.

"I know," I replied, turning toward him. When I looked at him, I realized that he was C. J. Blankenship. C.J. had transferred to Ocotillo sometime during sophomore year from Our Lady of Lourdes, one of the Catholic high schools in town. He had walked into sophomore English one day and had been assigned a seat on the other side of the room, so I never really talked to him. But all that was about to change.

"Allan, right?" he asked.

"Yeah, and you're C.J.," I said.

He snapped his fingers as if I'd just won a contest. "I wasn't sure you'd know my name," he said.

"Why not? We were in English together last year."

"I guess reporters just have a way with names and faces."

"Huh?"

"Don't you work on the school paper?"

"Well, yeah." Then I couldn't resist adding, "Only I'm feature editor this year, you know."

"I guess that makes you Big Man on Campus," he said.

I wasn't sure if I was getting a compliment or not. Even if I was, I hardly qualified for BMOC status, except in my dreams. "I don't know if anyone would agree with you about that," I said.

"You're kidding? You've got a great position on the paper. I bet lots of kids are jealous."

"You think so?" I asked, flattered at the thought.

"Definitely," he said. "With a position like that, you're going to get a lot of P.R. Who knows? You could be president of the student council next year."

"No, not quite. I'm not exactly the president type."

"Don't sell yourself short," he said. "You never know. Anyway, one thing's for sure, you'll be able to get into any college you want. Unless you're planning on going to ASU." Arizona State University was ten miles away, a commuter's paradise for kids who didn't want to leave home.

"No, I want to go out of state," I explained. "Maybe to Kansas or Missouri. They have good journalism schools."

"That's a good idea," he said. "Out of state is definitely the place to be."

"Where are you going to apply?"

He shrugged and said, "I haven't even thought about it. But I know that once I cross that Arizona border, I'm never coming back. I didn't want to come back this year. It's so hard to be here now."

"What do you mean?"

"I mean, how would you feel if you spent the summer in New York City? Would you want to come home? Or would you want to stay in New York?"

"You did? You spent the summer there? Doing what?"

"Living there," he said, as if it was the most natural thing to do. "Believe me, it was a lot better than being here. Don't you ever get sick of Phoenix? It's such a hick town. You know, there's never anything to do here," he explained. "Everything shuts down at nine o'clock. There're never any good movies. You read a review of some movie in *Time*, and it takes a year to get here. There're just too many old people here; they all want to watch *Donahue* and catch the tenth showing of *The Sound of Music*."

I had to agree with that. Phoenix was loaded with senior citizens. I nodded and said, "I know what you mean."

"You should really go there sometime. To New York, I mean."

"Yeah, one day, maybe," I said.

He was silent a moment, then he asked, "Well, what about Columbia?"

"What about it?" I asked dumbly. I wasn't sure what Columbia he meant.

"Columbia University, New York City. Big journalism school. I guess you've ruled it out?"

I looked at him and almost laughed from nervousness. He made me feel as if I were settling for second—or even third—best.

"Don't sell yourself short," he advised. "That's one way you could get to New York. Right?" I didn't know what to say. "Right?" he insisted.

"Well, yeah, right," I managed finally.

"Have *you* thought about going to Columbia?" I asked him.

"Possibly, but I'm leaving the door open for now. And that's what you should do."

"What are you going to major in? Or haven't you decided yet?"

"International relations," he announced proudly. "Then I'm going to be the president of my own consulting firm and live in New York. Who knows? We could even run into each other, after you graduate from Columbia."

"Yeah, maybe," I said, considering his suggestion. Somehow, C.J. was painting a tempting picture of the future in my mind.

OCOTILLO WHIZ AWARDED SCHOLARSHIP TO COLUMBIA

I could see it all. I'd graduate and end up with a job at the *New York Times*. C.J. would come to New York and start his firm. We could even be roommates.

It was at that moment that I realized I had found a friend.

"What classes are you taking anyway?" I asked. He pulled out his schedule and handed it to me. "We have English and American History together third and fourth hour," I said, returning his schedule. "Maybe that'll make Briggs bearable."

"Nothing could help that prune," C.J. said. "Except early retirement, or a terminal disease."

I laughed.

"We'll have to eat lunch together," he continued. "But I've got some errands today. Maybe tomorrow. That way I can work on getting you to think about Columbia."

When the bell rang, C.J. stayed right with me as we walked to English, as if we had known each other for years. He was just

the friend I had been looking for; he was intelligent, sophisticated and a little daring. Besides, he told me everything I
wanted to hear.

Chapter Five

We had no sooner walked into junior English with Mrs. Briggs and sat down, than Sandra Parker spotted me.

"Hi, Allan," she called.

I blanched. "Hi, Sandra."

Then she waddled right up to me, and I cringed.

PIG SUFFOCATES TEEN

English Class Watches in Horror!

"I didn't know we were going to be in the same class," she said. With that, she sat right behind me. Then she continued, in that cute voice of hers, "I got your present today."

C.J. glanced at me, a curious look on his face.

Without looking at Sandra, I nodded and thought about hiding under my desk.

"Did anyone ever tell you that you have the longest eye lashes?" she asked.

I wanted to die.

"A lot of girls would kill for your lashes. I guess I'm just noticing them now because of your contacts. You look really good in them, you know."

"Thanks," I mumbled, hoping she would shut up before C.J. thought we were friends or something.

Then the bell rang, and Briggs tried to call the class to order.

Sandra leaned forward and whispered, "This is going to be boring."

I nodded slightly.

"It's too bad we need this to graduate," she added.

"Yeah," I muttered, hoping C.J. didn't see Sandra whisper in my ear.

"What kind of present did you buy Sandra Parker?" C.J. asked me after class. "An apple to stuff in her mouth?"

"I didn't buy her anything," I said. "I just gave her back something that was hers."

"What? Her virginity?"

"Come on," I prompted. The last thing I wanted to talk about was Sandra and sex.

"Well, what was it?" he asked.

I sighed. "Eye shadow."

"Eye shadow? I'd hate to think how you got that."

I was blushing by then. "It's not what you think."

"So who said anything?" he replied. "I didn't say anything, did I?"

"You didn't have to," I said, looking around to make sure she wasn't nearby.

"Did you see how big she was?"

I thought I should be agreeing with him, but I found myself saying, "She's not that big."

"Face it, Allan," C.J. countered, "if you filled her full of helium and put Goodyear on her side, you know what you'd have."

I laughed in spite of myself and kept walking.

C.J. and I moved on to American History then and sat dumbfounded through a fifty-minute lecture on the discovery of America. I took five pages of notes and ended up with a case of writer's cramp. But that was Mr. Hancock for you. After class C.J. told me he'd see me tomorrow and we'd eat lunch together.

"If you don't have errands," I mimicked. "Right?"

"Right," he said, and smiled. "You learn fast," he added. "I like that."

After I exchanged my books for my lunch sack at my locker, I decided to sit at one of the most accessible tables in the cafeteria in hopes that someone exciting might want to sit with me. I sat there, pretending that I was waiting for someone to show up. I could see Sandra Parker chowing down a few tables over, but fortunately she hadn't seen me.

"Mind if I eat with you?" It was Harry, trying to be funny.

I shrugged and kept eating.

"We must not have any classes together this year," he said, sitting opposite me.

"I guess not. I have Spanish and journalism this afternoon."

"Yeah, I have German and typing," he said. "So what do you have for lunch today?" he asked. This was typical. He always bought his lunch, but he still wanted to know what I had in my brown bag. He picked up my lunch sack and peered in. "Oreos. My favorites."

He told me that every time I brought Oreos for dessert. The same Old Harry was driving the New Allan crazy.

"What'd you do this summer?" Harry asked.

"Not much," I said. "I got contacts."

"You did?" he asked, sounding surprised.

"Don't you remember? I used to wear glasses."

"Oh, yeah, I guess." He stopped to take a bite, then said, "My dad sent me to tennis camp in Tucson. I was there for two months."

"That's nice," I said.

"I really improved my game," he continued. "I was thinking about going out for the tennis team this fall."

I could just see Harry running all over the court, swinging at air. I smiled and took another bite of my sandwich.

"Hey, did you hear what happened to Hancock during third hour American History?"

"No." In the distance I watched Sandra Parker chewing her sandwich. "What?"

"I just about died. He was playing with a rubber band while he was talking. You know how he is when he's nervous."

"They don't call him Spastic Joe for nothing," I offered. All of the kids called him Spastic Joe because he was always dropping everything, ranging from paper clips to books to—as the famous story went—the blackboard one day.

"Well, he flipped a rubber band and hit Theresa Kline."

"Yeah?" While I waited for the punch line, I observed Sandra biting into an apple.

"It went right up her skirt. You know how she sits."

"I can't believe it! What'd everyone do?" I asked. "They must've cracked up."

"Yeah, that's the—"

I heard a loud smooching sound. Without thinking, I looked up at Brian's smirking face as he walked by with a few other football jocks. "Ribbit," he croaked. As he passed, I glanced at Sandra Parker, who was looking right at me.

"Damn it," I managed. That would teach me to be interested in anything Harry had to say again. I just wanted to disappear.

"What're you so mad about?"

"Brian Sawyer," I told him. "Don't you ever notice what he does?"

Harry shook his head. "He doesn't bother me."

"Didn't you hear him ribbit when he went by? He just does it to make fun of me—of us."

"Why?" Sometimes Harry could be really dense.

"Forget it. Well, at least he won't be in my Spanish class this year. I think Castillo gave him an *F* last year."

"Let's go to the library," Harry suggested. I think this was his way of appeasing me. "I've got to catch up on all the magazines I missed over the summer."

I didn't want to tag along with Harry, but the last thing I wanted was to stay in the cafeteria now that Brian had spotted us. As I stuffed my trash into my lunch sack, Harry continued, "Do you want a ride home tonight?"

I felt like screaming. Why was he being so nice?

"Well—"

"We can stop at A&W if you want," he volunteered. A&W had been our official hangout. No one popular ever went there.

"Well—"

Why couldn't I just say no?

"I, uh—"

I wanted a girlfriend, I told myself. I didn't want to hang around with Harry.

"I've got to buy the rest of my books," he continued. "I'll meet you in the bookstore after school."

I watched him looking at me. I could be the New Allan and say no, that I had other plans, that I didn't need to be friends any more. But the Old Allan wasn't sure what other plans I had or if I'd ever make a new friend. Maybe C.J. had enough friends already. And maybe no girl would ever be interested in me, contacts or not.

"Hey, Allan," Harry said, waving his hand in front of my eyes. "Are you there? Do you want a ride or not?"

"Okay," I said finally, as the Old Allan took control of my body.

Chapter Six

When I walked into Mrs. Castillo's classroom that afternoon, I saw my seat immediately, near the front on the far side, behind the beautiful blonde.

"Are you saving this for anyone?" I asked her, pointing to the empty desk.

With her green eyes, she looked at me long enough before answering that I began to blush.

"For you," she said, as if she had chosen me especially.

I lost my breath for a second, then tried to regain my composure. I thought, *You're saving it for me?* I wanted to ask her if she knew who I was, but I stopped myself again. *For me?* I asked myself again. *She's saving the seat for me?* She didn't even know me. I saw the perfect headline:

> GOD ANSWERS TEEN'S PRAYERS,
> SENDS BLONDE TO FROG EYES

The miracle girl turned out to be Sue Arnold, a transfer student from Chandler, Arizona.

"You can sit down, you know," she told me after I had asked who she was.

I must have looked like a moron, waiting for a pigeon to land on my head. I sat down and tried to think of something to say.

"What's this class like?" she asked.

"Not too bad," I told her. "If you do the work, it's easy. What else are you taking?"

"Nothing else with you, I bet," she said as if she minded terribly.

"You don't have journalism next hour, do you?"

"Typing," she said. "I like to take it last hour, so I don't fall asleep. Have you ever tried to fall asleep while you were typing?"

I laughed. "Not really."

"Well, don't ever try," she said, bending and straightening her right index finger. It looked so perfect with its pointy little nail. "That's what happened when I took typing first hour once. I fell asleep and caught my finger between the return and shift keys. I don't recommend it."

I was hanging on every word she said. "What *do* you recommend?" I asked.

"It depends on what you want," she said in mock seriousness.

"Want? Well, nothing," I said quickly. "I—I just meant—I thought you meant—"

Then she smiled, and I stopped talking. I told myself then that Sue had enormous potential to be my first real girlfriend. She wasn't one of the Home Ec types I usually dated, who gave me the driest, thinnest kisses you could imagine. And she was new enough not to know about Frog Eyes.

By the end of the period I was sure that my plan would work. I'd wait a few weeks, get to know Sue, then ask her out.

Goodbye, Harry.

Goodbye, Brian.

Hello, Sue.

I walked into journalism next hour just in time to hear Vicky Lincoln ask Ginger D'Angelo if she was going to Norm Bukowski's party that Saturday. For two years I had been hearing Vicky ask Ginger (and Ginger ask Vicky) about mutual parties they had attended or were planning to attend, and I was jealous as hell.

"Maybe," Ginger said. "Maybe not."

"Well, what else would you do?" Vicky asked.

"Greg and I might go to the Party House instead," Ginger said matter-of-factly.

"You liar!" Vicky said. "You don't even know where it is."

"Neither do you, Lincoln."

"I know everything," Vicky teased.

The Party House, an infamous place around Phoenix, supposedly held parties at all hours every night. Free food, booze, drugs and sex. The only problem was that no one at school knew where the House was or whether it really existed, or if they did, they weren't talking to me.

"Is that where your new boyfriend is taking you?" Ginger continued.

Vicky pursed her lips and looked innocent. "What new boyfriend?"

"Whoever you've been dating for the last month."

"If it's news, I'll put it in my column," Vicky replied.

Vicky was the *Observer*'s resident gossip columnist who wrote "The Observing Eye."

"Allan!" Vicky yelled a moment later. "You got new eyes! Let me see." She stared up at my brown eyes while I blushed. I had had a crush on Vicky ever since we both began working on the *Observer* freshman year. In fact, I got itchy every time she was near me. "Ginger, look at Allan's lashes! They're so long! I think they're longer than yours, D'Angelo."

Ginger moved in to stare at my eyes, too.

"Now maybe your dent'll go away," Vicky told me.

"What dent?" I asked, as panic set in. If she hadn't been staring at me, I would've checked my fly.

"The dent on the bridge of your nose. Now stand still and quit fidgeting. Right here," she said, tapping the space between my eyes. I practically jumped when she touched me. "You can see where your glasses used to be."

"You can?" Why hadn't I ever noticed it before?

"They must've been really heavy," Ginger said.

"They didn't call him Frog Eyes for nothing," Vicky teased. "Now you'll need a new nickname."

"How about Allan?" I said.

"Don't worry," she said, and winked. "I'll think of a good one, just in case you ever break into my column."

Breaking into Vicky's column was what school and popularity were all about. Vicky knew all the right people at school, and she didn't mind telling everyone what the right people were doing. I would've thought that they'd be angry about her column, but Vicky couldn't have been more popular if she tried. She was great at picking up on everyone else's gossip, although you'd never find anything about her in "The Eye." For some reason, she was tight-lipped about her own social life. But I knew three things about her: she smoked Marlboros, she liked to park on Camelback Mountain, and she had had at least three serious boyfriends. Whenever I was around Vicky, all I could think about was Camelback Mountain and those three lucky guys.

"What're you doing Friday night?" Ginger asked then.

"Oh, I don't know," she said. "Maybe I'll just stay home."

"What happened to Ed?" I asked before I could stop myself. She had been dating Ed Conroy last May.

Vicky looked a little surprised. "None of your bee's wax, Allan. I'm not going out with him now."

"There's a mystery man in her life," Ginger added, more to needle Vicky than to inform me.

"Let's get to work, people," Miss Compton ordered, before I could imagine who the mystery man might be. She was standing at the door that separated her classroom from the journalism workroom. "The first issue is coming out on Friday, and all copy goes to the printer by tomorrow morning. Let's get on it."

I quickly moved away from Vicky as if she was contagious and buried myself in my work. I had decided to write an account of some students' summer exploits in a what-I-did-over-summer-vacation article. Two Ocotillo students had spent the summer in Zaire and Japan on a foreign-exchange program, and I had heard that Bob Brennan rafted down the Colorado. Then it occurred to me that C.J.'s summer in New York might make good material for the story, too. I remembered that he had trig sixth hour, and I decided to meet him when class let out.

"Oh, Allan, can you come up to my desk for a moment?" the Comp asked. We called her that for short sometimes.

I followed her to the front of the classroom.

"Allan," she said, sitting at her desk, "I've got some good news for you. I had a call from the *Register* this afternoon. You've been chosen as Ocotillo's teen correspondent."

"You're kidding?" I said, stunned by the news.

"Your first story is due next Friday night after the game," she continued. "They're going to send you a style sheet and writing tips and all the other information. But you're not going to let this interfere with your work on the *Observer*, are you? I'd hate to see your writing suffer."

That was the Comp for you. She no sooner told you the good news than she followed it up with her own kind of threat. Being selected as teen correspondent was a feather in my cap, but I had my work cut out for me. Mostly, it meant that I'd cover all of Ocotillo's home football and basketball games and phone in a story and the statistics after the games. It also meant that I could write occasional articles for the Saturday morning teen correspondent page in the *Register*.

In the short run, it meant that I'd be more popular at school. In the long run, it meant that I was finally hitting the big time.

School was turning out just the way I wanted.

After I finished working on my story that hour, I had just enough time to collect my books and make it to C.J.'s trig class before the bell rang. C.J. was the first person out the door.

"What's up?" he asked when he saw me.

"Well, I'm writing this article on what some kids did over summer vacation and I wanted to include your summer in New York, only I needed some more information. Do you have time now? Can I ask you some questions?"

"No comment," he announced, as if he was some kind of politician.

"No, really—"

"No comment," he repeated.

"C.J., stop joking. I—"

"I'm not joking," he said, "not really. I just don't want to be in the story."

"Why? Everyone'd be really impressed with your summer."

"They'll just come up and ask me all about it. I don't want to relive it for the masses. It's hard enough to adjust to being back."

"But—"

"You can write another story about me sometime. I do all kinds of interesting things," he said, then smiled. "Hey, do you want a ride? I've got my car."

I almost laughed out loud. I couldn't believe my luck.

"Sure, right now?" He nodded. "It must be nice to have your own car."

As we walked outside, we passed the bookstore on our way to the parking lot. I wasn't sure what to do, so I did nothing. I didn't look for Harry even though the front of the store had two large plate-glass windows. I held my head straight and stared at the horizon as we started past.

But then there was Harry running out of the bookstore, making an ass of himself.

"Hey, Allan!" he yelled. "My car's out front!"

I turned around, not focusing on him, and waved him off as casually as I could. "That's okay, Harry, I'm on assignment." I turned back around, and C.J. and I continued walking toward the parking lot.

"Who's that?" C.J. asked.

"An old friend," I said. "But we're not really friends anymore."

C.J. smiled at me knowingly, then drove me home in his Toyota.

Chapter Seven

After that first day of school, my hopes for the New Allan were high. I had become teen correspondent, I had a new friend and, with C.J.'s help, I was able to avoid Harry like the plague. C.J. and I ate lunch together the rest of the week, but instead of eating inside, we ate outside on the patio, far away from Harry's lonely table. I knew that if I played my cards right, I'd have a blond girlfriend and more popularity in no time.

Saturday morning I had finished my breakfast when Rich walked through the kitchen on his way to the garage, carrying his sheets to the washer. I couldn't miss the distinctive odor, even if it was probably the first time in three or four months that he had wet the bed.

I waited with my mother and the Duke at the breakfast bar, while Rich stuffed them in the washer. None of us said anything. Rich was embarrassed enough that my mother and the Duke didn't want to make him feel more ashamed. I just wondered if he thought about wetting the bed every night before he went to sleep, but I kept my mouth shut.

As he walked back into the family room, Rich acted very casual, despite the embarrassment. He had a special code worked out with my mother, so he didn't even have to discuss it.

"My sheets are in the washer," he told her. That was the signal.

"I'll get to them later today," she said.

Mission accomplished, Rich was off to school for his JV game.

"Why don't you make him do his own laundry?" I asked two seconds after he had left the house. "Maybe he'd stop wetting the bed that way."

"Allan, this is between Rich, your father and me," my mother said.

"But, Mom, you guys baby him so much," I said.

"Sometimes Rich needs some extra attention," the Duke added.

"If I wet my bed, you'd kill me," I reminded him.

"That's right," the Duke agreed.

"Then why don't you do the same thing to Rich?"

"Allan," my mother began, "you and Rich are different from each other, so we treat you differently."

"Well, I don't think it's fair," I commented.

"We didn't think you would," the Duke replied. "So you notice that we didn't ask you."

Then the phone rang.

"Hello?" I answered.

"Is this the famous sports celebrity?" the female voice said.

"What?"

"I am speaking to the famous *Register* sportswriter, aren't I? Allan Antottle?"

Then I knew. "Is this who I think it is?"

"I don't know," the cute voice said. "It depends on who you think it is."

"Sandra?"

"Of course, silly. Only it's Sandy," she corrected. "Remember?"

"I was just walking out the door," I lied, trying to end the conversation. "I've got some stuff to do."

"Well, I won't keep you. I just wanted to call to say that I saw your picture in the paper today."

"You did?"

"Page seventeen. You're there with all the other teen correspondents."

"I guess Miss Compton sent my picture in. I'll have to look as soon as I get off the phone."

"I thought you were walking out the door," she teased.

"Well, I was," I said, thinking fast, "but I can take a minute to look in the paper."

"When do you write your first story?"

"This Friday. I only get to write the home games," I said.

"Maybe when they see how good a job you do on the home games, they'll let you write the away games, too."

"I don't think so," I said, "but it's a nice idea."

"Well, I won't keep you. I know you're busy." Then she said, in her cutest, skinniest voice, "I'll see you Monday, Mr. Correspondent."

When I hung up the phone, I thought I'd be glad to be rid of her. And I was, only another part of me wanted to keep talking to her. But I didn't stop to figure out why. I grabbed the paper and turned to page seventeen.

By midafternoon, my parents had gone to watch Rich's JV game. Home alone, I tried to work on some story ideas, but something kept nagging at me. I knew exactly what it was; I just didn't want to admit it. The New Allan may have done all of the right things so far, but the Old Allan's mind was still in charge. And the Old Allan had a lot of things he worried about, like what was going to happen in P.E. on Monday, the day we began our first unit, swimming.

There were two reasons I dreaded swimming. In the first place, I didn't know how to swim. My parents had forced me to take swimming lessons when I was little. While everyone else was swimming the length of the pool, I was lucky to take four strokes before swallowing water and gagging. I simply couldn't master the logistics of stroking and breathing. But then, I had a coordination problem in all sports.

I was also embarrassed by my body, once I had "matured."
As my body changed and as hair seemed to sprout in places I
least wanted it, I became self-conscious. The fact that at four-
teen I had hair on my chest didn't help any, especially when
none of the other boys did. At sixteen, I was a veteran turf
farmer. I had enough chest hair for a million hair transplants
if I ever went bald. I was the only boy I knew who wore an undershirt in Phoenix during the summer. An undershirt in 120-
degree weather? I suffered because of my genes.

The funny thing was that I didn't get the hair genes from my
father, who had a chest that was as smooth as a baby's behind
and who was going bald, if the wind blew in the right direction. He used to tease me by saying things like, "You'd better
eat your crust (I hated crust!). It'll put hair on your chest."
Actually, I think he was jealous of me, but that didn't make me
feel any better.

So I put down my pen and notepad and did something I
swore I was never going to do again. I put on my swimming suit
and stared at myself in the full-length mirror in my parents'
bedroom. This was me, this was my (hairy) body. This was
something that I shouldn't be self-conscious about. Only, I
didn't know how to get all of that to sink in through my thick
skull. How was I ever going to make it through the unit? The
school thought it was doing juniors a big favor by saving the
swimming unit till junior year. All that meant was that my Day
of Reckoning was finally at hand.

I grabbed a bath towel and practiced draping it over my
shoulder. Which way looked better? But no matter what I did,
I looked like a dork. I tried to walk with a swagger, but my arms
kept trying to cover my chest.

"What're you doing?"

My mother was standing in the doorway, looking as if she
had just found out I was gay or something. I turned twenty
shades of red and pulled the towel around my neck.

"Nuh—nothing." I felt like such a fool.

"Allan—"

"I, uh, just wanted to see if my swimming suit still fits," I said, aware that the dam had opened and sweat was pouring down my sides. "We have swimming in P.E. on Monday."

"Oh, okay," she said, believing me immediately. "You don't have to act so self-conscious about it."

I decided to change the subject. "Why're you home? Is the game over?" I asked as I walked across the room to the door.

"No, your father's there. I needed to get something I forgot. We have to go to The Broadway after the game, so I can return a skirt I bought last week. I just came home to get it."

I got out of there fast.

A little later, I had recovered enough to work on story ideas again. I glanced through the small, first issue that had come out Friday afternoon. Not much was in it, except a few sports stories, a rundown on fall events and Vicky's column. She had obviously had a busy summer—snooping: someone who dates R.F. should know better than to go up on Camelback Mountain and "park" in a no parking zone; an unnamed cheerleader's bed was shortsheeted at cheerleading camp; members of the football team decided to cool off at Saguaro Lake by skinny-dipping, etc. It was a typical Vicky column, and everyone loved it. I couldn't help but wonder if I'd ever be popular enough—and do something daring enough—to be included.

I was making a list of possible stories for future issues, when I heard the front door open and Rich's voice boom through the house.

"We won," he called and walked quickly down the hallway. As he passed my door, he looked in.

"I scored two TD's," he bragged. "Lamont threw a fifty-yard pass to me in the end zone in the last minute. Can you believe it?"

I barely grunted, without looking up.

"What're you doing?" he asked.

I was working on a story, but I told him, "Not much."

He walked into my room then. "Patti Johnson was so happy that she couldn't wait to go out with me afterwards," he said, craning his neck to the left, showing off a trio of hickeys under his right ear. I was amazed. It wasn't even nighttime. How did you get a girl to kiss you like that during the day?

"Who's Patti Johnson?" I asked him.

"A freshman."

"She goes to OHS?" I asked.

He nodded. "She can suck like a vampire," he said proudly. "She's really something."

"I bet she is," I replied, feeling so jealous that I wished twenty hickeys would appear on my neck.

SEES DAYLIGHT HICKEYS,
VIRGIN TEEN GOES BERSERK

As soon as I visualized the headline, I knew I was going to have to work even faster if I was going to make changes. I lay back on my bed and began to plot my plan of attack.

"Who's calling, please?" the alien voice asked after dinner that night. I was putting my plan into action.

"Oh, uh, this is Allan." I paused and, as if to defend myself, added, "I sit behind her in Spanish class."

The phone clunked onto a hard surface.

Then I heard someone say, *"Buenos noches, señor."*

I couldn't believe it. "Huh—hi."

"What're you up to tonight?" Sue asked.

"Not much. I was wondering, could, I mean, can you go out with me? To the game?"

She didn't hesitate one second. "Sure. That'd be nice. What time is it? I don't know if I can get ready in time."

"It's not tonight," I blurted. "It's next Friday. There's never a game on Saturday, unless it's during basketball season, and then there aren't that many of them, because they play on Tuesday, too."

"What?" She was laughing at me then.

"Oh, well, I have to study some more, so I'll talk to you about it Monday. Okay? So we'll go out Friday?"

It was only after I hung up the phone that I realized she thought I was asking her for a date that night. I could have gone out with her—just like that—if I hadn't been so nervous. I wanted to kick myself.

Instead, I asked for the car.

"That's Friday night?" the Duke clarified.

"Yes," I said impatiently.

"Both of the cars'll be tied up," he said. "We have a dinner party Friday night. And I have an appointment to take the Ford into the body shop on Thursday." He and Mom had been in two fender benders that they had neglected to have fixed. "It'll be in there all weekend."

"But can't you wait to take it in?" I asked. "I really need to use it."

"I've waited too long already," he said. "And I've had the appointment for two weeks now."

"But what am I going to do?"

"You'll just have to find another way."

"But I've already asked her. How am I going to take her out?"

"Allan, you've got yourself a problem," the Duke said. "You should've checked with us before you asked her out." His common sense approach to life never made any sense to me until it was too late. "Is that so hard?"

"Okay, I'm checking now. Can I use the Buick a week from Friday?"

"Yes, you can use one of the cars," the Duke said, then added, "if you're nice."

"We could give you and Sue a ride to the game," my mother volunteered. "What about that?"

"Mom, we're not in sixth grade. Forget it. Good night," I said, and marched down the hall to my room.

I was starting to get undressed for bed later, when I heard Rich call down the hall to the family room, "Where're my sheets, Mom?"

She didn't answer right away, probably because she was reading subtitles. She and my father had rented some French movie for the VCR.

"Mom," Rich prompted.

"On the line," she said finally.

"Well, aren't you going to make my bed?"

"Richard, I'm trying to watch this. You know how to do it."

"But, Mom—" he whined.

She didn't answer.

"Mom—"

"All right," she said, relenting. "But not till the movie's over."

That was their idea of fairness: they'd make his bed, but they wouldn't let me use the car. I wished they'd let us both grow up.

Chapter Eight

Monday morning I had one thing on my mind, finding a ride for Friday night. But that worry was temporarily derailed as soon as I walked into the bathhouse first hour, carrying my swimsuit. I wasn't looking forward to P.E. that day, but I had managed to start believing that swimming and self-conscious anxiety weren't going to kill me. That is, until I saw Brian Sawyer at the far end of the locker area.

He was joking around with a couple of basketball players. From somewhere he had gotten a large stick shaped like a Y. Around the top two prongs he had wrapped the bands of his athletic supporter, using the cup as a slingshot. I watched him put a Red Delicious apple in the cup and shoot it across the locker room, where it thudded against some lockers and left a smear of pulp as it dropped to the floor. Even though he wasn't aiming in my direction, I gulped and froze anyway.

"Get in line for your locker assignments," Coach Mac-Addino yelled. Coaches were just like cops as far as I was concerned; they were never there when you needed them. I headed for the back of the forming line, well-separated from Brian.

Leon Graves, who was the statistician for the football team, was in front of me. "What's Sawyer doing here?" I asked, since I knew that football players were excused from regular P.E.

"He got axed from the team," Leon whispered. "Broke training."

"How?"

"Out after curfew," Leon confided. "And smoking."

"Smoking?" Half the football team smoked.

Leon nodded. "Can you believe it? Coach saw him Thursday night around eleven o'clock at Pizza Hut, smoking. Two violations, so he kicked him off the team. Just like that."

"How long's he out for?"

"The season. Coach won't take him back."

Brian Sawyer was angry enough as a normal person without losing his position on the football team. Now I knew I was in real trouble.

After lockers were assigned, we changed into our swimsuits and were told to meet outside on the deck of the pool. I pulled my suit as high as it would go, then flung my towel over my shoulder. As I walked outside into the sunny pool area, Brian was already in the water, holding onto the side drain.

"Where's Harry, hairy?" he called, as I walked onto the deck. It was a combination I had never considered, and it made me mad. Didn't he know that I wasn't friends with Harry anymore?

"Hey, hairy," he repeated. I looked down, and self-consciousness overwhelmed me; the sunshine magnified every follicle. I tried to stand in back of some guys, so he couldn't see me. I wanted to blend in with the background and disappear from his warped sight, but I kept imagining the worst.

HUMILIATED BY BULLY, HAIRY TEEN DROWNS IN HIGH SCHOOL POOL

Then the coach walked out of the bathhouse. "Sawyer, I said to wait on the deck. Get out of there on the double!"

"But Coach—" Brian was full of mock sincerity.

"You heard me!"

Brian hoisted himself out of the pool.

"Okay, now, I want all of you, except Mr. Sawyer, to stand at the edge of the pool. I'll tell you when to get in," the coach said. "Sawyer, you stand right here with me."

I started to walk to the pool's edge, well away from Brian, when I realized I still had my contacts in.

"Now, slowly, fellows, get in the pool," the coach commanded. "And I don't want any splashing!"

I was panicking. I couldn't wear my contacts in the pool.

"Antottle, what're you waiting for?"

I blushed, crossed my arms for protection, and walked over to him. "Coach, I got contacts—I mean, I forgot to bring my case—for my contacts—I can't get them wet. I'll bring it tomorrow."

"I swim in mine all the time," he said.

"You have contacts?"

"Now get in there!" he ordered.

"But my optometrist said not to, and if I lost one, my father'd kill me."

"Okay, if that's how you want it. You and Sawyer can run fifty laps around the pool."

"But—"

"Start moving, you two." I started to run in the opposite direction from Brian. "This way, Antottle!" the Coach directed. "You two can keep pace. Fifty laps, let's go!"

I turned around and caught up with Brian.

"Way to go, hairy," he said.

I ignored him and kept running.

After I showered, I practically ran from the locker room. Even then I could hear Brian saying in his distinctive mocking tone, "Where's Harry, hairy?" I was going to do something about it, but first I had to find a ride for my date with Sue.

I decided to try C.J. in homeroom.

"You going to the game Friday?" I asked him.

"Maybe, why?"

"Oh, well, it's just that Sue and I were going out and I thought you might want to double with us."

"Hmm—" He sounded interested.

"The only problem is that you'd need to drive, because our cars are tied up for Friday night. Or I'd drive otherwise."

His eyes were moving as if he was trying to read something inside his head. "Yeah, that's right," he said, finally looking at me. "How could I forget? I have plans, so I can't go. Maybe some other time."

"What're you doing?" I asked, trying not to sound nosey.

"Oh, I'm flying to L.A.," he said.

"What?"

"Faye is taking me to L.A. this weekend," he said, as if I should know who Faye was. I'm sure I looked totally confused, but he continued, "One of her little shopping expeditions."

"Who's Faye?" I asked finally.

"She's my aunt. Aunt Faye. I thought I told you about her. You'll have to meet her sometime."

"Yeah," I said, still wondering what I was going to do.

Then C.J. continued, "I know, you'll have to come with us. Not this weekend, but sometime soon. Aunt Faye keeps talking about going to Santa Fe one weekend. Have you ever been there?" I shook my head. "Well, I'll let you know if and when—usually she likes to go on the spur of the moment, so keep a suitcase packed."

"Your parents don't mind?"

He didn't miss a beat. "Why should they?" he asked. "Faye is so great. She's my father's sister. She's lived all over the world. Really, she's just like a good friend." Then he added, "You really will have to come with us when we go to Santa Fe. All these movie stars have homes there now. We'll go to a real fancy place to eat. I'm telling you, Aunt Faye'll knock you out."

I turned around then and tried to delve into *The Scarlet Letter* for Briggs, but the thought of going to Santa Fe one weekend kept interfering. By the time I graduated I would be just as sophisticated as C.J.

* * *

The answer to my transportation problem came at lunch. C.J. said he had some errands to do, so I capitalized on his absence. I bypassed the patio and went directly into the cafeteria. Harry was sitting in the far corner by himself, and Brian was nowhere in sight.

"I haven't seen you since school started," I told him as I joined him at the table.

"Yeah." He sounded annoyed.

"Junior year is so busy. They never tell you how busy you're going to be."

"I know," Harry said, shoveling some chili con carnage. "I've been concentrating on my tennis. They have tryouts for the team next week."

"Well, good luck," I said. "You know, we're going to have to get together sometimes and go out. Like last year."

"Yeah," he mumbled, still chewing.

I added, "We could double or something."

He looked up at me then. "Yeah, maybe."

"Well, why don't we start arranging something? What about this Friday? Is that too soon?" I asked, looking him in the eye.

"Well, yeah, that'd be okay," he said. "Can you get a date between now and then?"

I almost laughed. "Oh, it's only Tuesday. That's plenty of time. Can't you?"

"I think so," he said. "I'll have to see."

"Great—then it's all fixed. We'll double on Friday."

"Okay," he said, sounding more at ease.

"How're your classes? I really haven't seen you around. I can't believe we don't have any together." I got him talking about himself when lunch was almost over, I added the finishing touch, "Why don't you take my Oreos? I don't feel like eating them today."

"Are you sure?" Harry asked, as if I had offered him a thousand dollars.

"Yeah." Then I paused. "Well, good luck getting a date. You can get the car, can't you?"

"Didn't you know?" he asked. Then he announced, in a tone guaranteed to make me jealous, "I have my own car now."

"You do?" I said, trying to act unimpressed. "I thought you had to use your mother's."

"She made my dad buy me one. She said as long as he wrecked the marriage, he was going to pay for it. So she made him get me a new Pontiac. I got it last weekend."

"That's great," I forced myself to say. At least I could look forward to my date with Sue.

In Spanish that afternoon I told her we were going to double.

"Who with?" she asked.

"Harry Snyder."

"I don't think I know him. Who's he taking?"

"He doesn't know yet," I told her. "It'll be someone we know, I'm sure. They'll be good company for you."

"Oh, I don't care about them," she said. "You'll be there."

"Oh, but, d-don't you remember?" I asked, trying to remember myself if I had told her. "I'm teen correspondent, and I cover all the home games for the *Register*. So I have to be in the press box during the game. Didn't I tell you?"

She just looked at me.

"But I'll be with you at halftime," I said. "Then we can go out for a pizza afterwards—and then, you know, whatever—"

"With Harry and Whoever," she added. I couldn't tell if she was making a joke or not.

"I really meant to tell you. I thought I did."

"That's okay," she said. "I didn't know you were this big newspaper reporter."

"Well, I don't know if I'd say 'big' or anything," I said, watching her face for any sign of disappointment. "But it's part of the job."

If she was disappointed, she didn't show it. In fact, we didn't mention the date for the rest of the week.

Chapter Nine

The rest of the week, Brian ribbeted and teased me about my chest and Harry, but all I thought about was my date with Sue. Going out with her would be sheer heaven. I couldn't wait to see what she'd be like on a date, how she'd act, whether she'd hold hands with me or let me put my arm around me, whether she'd kiss me good-night. I figured that we'd park somewhere after the game and with just Sue and me in the back seat, we could disappear from Harry's rearview mirror.

BACK SEAT SEX!
Teen Reporter Tells All

I was so anxious about my date with Sue that even the *Observer* didn't impress me when it was distributed sixth hour. And it wasn't often that I made Page One once, let alone twice. First, my summer vacation story had been printed on the lower right-hand part of the page. Next to that, boxed in, was an article announcing my selection as teen correspondent; the news editor had even used a small mug shot of me. I knew that was a good sign of my popularity, but a hot date with Sue would be even better.

When I got home from school that afternoon, I walked into the garage and tried to open the family room door, but it was locked. I knocked, figuring that Rich was home, but I heard nothing. Wondering where everyone was, I pulled out my keys and unlocked the door. A moment later, as I started into my bedroom, Rich came out of his bedroom and closed the door behind him.

"Why didn't you let me in?" I asked.

He just stood there.

"Where's Mom?" I tried again.

"She went to some fashion show at The Broadway."

"Who's making dinner?"

"You are," he announced.

"But I have a date. I don't have time for that."

"All I know is that Mom and Dad are going out to dinner. Mom said there's hamburger in the refrigerator, and you should make dinner."

"All right," I said. "I guess I can handle two hamburgers."

"You need to make enough for three," he said.

"Why? Are you eating for two these days?"

Then he grinned. "Hey, Patti, come on out."

His bedroom door opened, and Patti, who looked too scared to give hickeys, took a few reluctant steps forward. It was an awkward moment. Neither she nor I could look at each other, but Rich seemed to be enjoying his triumph.

"Patti's going to eat dinner here. Then we're going to the game."

I quickly retraced my route down the hall to the kitchen.

"Don't say anything about this, okay?" Rich asked, following me. I opened the refrigerator. "You wouldn't, would you?"

I grabbed a carton of yogurt and slammed the door. "I didn't see anything, but it'll cost you," I joked, even though I didn't want to. Now that I had a date with Sue, my little brother was still showing me up. I had my work cut out for me that night.

A few hours later, Harry picked me up fifteen minutes late.

"Where's your date?" I asked. "Who're you taking?" I had
bothered him about his date for the last three days. I had made
the supreme sacrifice of eating lunch with him instead of C.J.,
even though Brian Sawyer might spot us. But every time I asked
Harry who his date was, he kept shrugging it off, like he had
one in the bag.

"I don't have a date," he said.

"What?"

"I couldn't get one. I thought about asking Andrea Martin,
but I didn't call her till last night, and she had a date by then. I
didn't think you and Sue would mind. We can have a good
time."

I could see it all. Harry would sit beside Sue while I sat in the
press box, and she would hate every second of his company and
might end up hating me, too.

TEEN CORRESPONDENT KILLS EX-FRIEND
BLOND DATE WITNESSES BRUTAL MURDER

Then I thought of C.J., flying to L.A. with his aunt. Why
couldn't he have stayed in town? Didn't he know I needed his
help?

"I saw you on the front page," Harry said next, as if he were
trying to placate me. "Congratulations."

"Thanks," I muttered.

Why did Harry have to ruin everything?

At Sue's, as I escorted her to the car, I said, "Guess who
doesn't have a date?" She didn't answer. I opened the door for
her, and she slid in next to Harry.

"Hi, Sue. How are you?" he said.

"Fine," she answered, rather icily.

"Aren't you in Hancock's third-hour American History?"

"Yeah," she said.

"I thought you looked familiar," he told her.

"Let's go," I said, "or I'll be late."

Once at the game, Harry wouldn't leave us alone for a second so I could explain things to Sue. By then, it was almost
eight and I had to be in the press box to prepare my charts.

"Couldn't I come up there with you?" Sue asked.

"There's no extra room," I told her. "And anyway, no one else is allowed. But I wish you could."

Sue looked away, as if she hadn't heard, and sat next to Harry.

At halftime, I went into the stands with Sue and Harry, but, since Sue wasn't talking, Harry and I discussed the game. Right before I returned to the press box for the second half, I told Sue and Harry that I'd meet them at the car as soon as I could after the game.

"What do you mean?" she asked, finally saying something.

"I have to write a story and phone it into the *Register*."

"A whole story?" Sue asked.

"It's only a paragraph or two," I tried to reassure her. "It shouldn't take me longer than fifteen minutes or so."

I could hear her sigh as I walked away.

When the game was over, I ran to the dressing room and picked a spot in the coach's office to work on the final statistics. When I had the numbers, I quickly wrote a two-paragraph summary of the game, then phoned it in to one of the *Register*'s assistant sports editors. Right before I hung up, he asked my name for the byline.

"Hi, all finished," I said, getting into Harry's car. It was so quiet that I felt like I was getting into a hearse. "Sorry it took so long," I told Sue, "but the *Register*'s line was busy. I had to keep dialing. But I get my name in the paper tomorrow."

"Uh-huh," she replied, hardly moved at all.

"That's really great," Harry said.

"Why don't we get something to eat?" I volunteered. "I'm starved. Aren't you?" I asked Sue.

"Where do you want to go?" Harry asked.

"I don't care. What do you say, Sue?"

"It doesn't matter," she replied. "Where do you want to go, Harry?"

Harry wanted to go to Bob's Big Boy. There, the hostess asked for the number in our party, then eyed me suspiciously when I told her three. She led us to a small table near the back.

"What do you want?" I asked Sue.

"Give me a Big Boy Combination," Harry told the waitress. "And a cherry lime rickey."

Sue stared blankly at the menu.

"Do you know what you want?" I tried again.

"Nothing," Sue said. She closed the menu and handed it back to me.

"Nothing? Come on, you've got to get something." I realized the waitress was listening to everything. "Not even a Coke?"

"Okay, I'll have a Coke," she said.

"Sue," I pleaded, then told the waitress, "I'll take—we want—a Slim Jim, an order of fries and two large Cokes."

Then Harry announced that he was going to the bathroom and, standing up to leave, proceeded to spill his water glass on the paper Big Boy placemat. He quickly mopped it up with his napkin and left.

I seized the opportunity. "I'm sorry about tonight," I told Sue. "I didn't mean—"

"Don't even talk about it," she said.

"But—"

"I'll be back." She smiled weakly, then headed for the bathroom herself.

Our drinks arrived, and I poked at the ice in mine with my straw.

"Allan!"

It was Ginger D'Angelo.

"Hi," I said.

"Who're you with?" she asked, looking at the empty table.

"Sue Arnold and—" I saw Harry walk out of the bathroom and nodded in his direction "—him."

"That must be fun," she said, with a hint of sympathy.

"Who're you with?" I asked, fearing the worst.

"A bunch of kids," she said, as Harry sat down. "Including Greg, of course."

"Vicky and her mystery boyfriend?" I kidded.

"No, Vicky was busy tonight. I think she had to babysit," she explained. "She's missing a lot of fun, though. Teddy Wilcox and Brian Sawyer are doing their imitations of Mac-

Addino. Well, I better get to the little girls' room or they'll eat my food before I get back. Have a good time,'' she said, and winked at me.

Sue returned just as reticent as she left. Harry and I discussed the game until our food came, but I was only half listening to the conversation. I was more concerned about Brian, whom I had finally spotted near the front entrance. I would have to pass right by him as we left—and Harry would be tagging along.

Sue begrudgingly accepted a portion of my sandwich, nibbled on a few fries and drank part of her Coke. We were almost being civil to each other.

Then she asked Harry, "Do you really like that rickey thing?"

"Yeah," he answered seriously, "I like fruit drinks."

Sue and I snickered. The bond between us was tentatively established again.

"You want to taste it?" he asked her.

She wrinkled her nose.

"It won't kill you," he said, offering her the drink.

I figured Sue wouldn't want "Harry germs," but she leaned over and took a brief sip through his straw.

"Well?" he asked.

She shrugged. "It's not as weird as I thought it'd be," she said.

Harry seemed pleased, and I was relieved that Sue was finally warming up.

"Well, you ready?" Harry asked when we were through.

"Don't you want dessert?" I asked, hoping to stall till Ginger and her friends left.

"Not this weekend. If I'm going out for the tennis team on Monday, I don't want to fill up on sweets," he said. "That's not good for my game."

"You're going out for tennis?" Sue asked. Harry nodded. "I was on the girls' JV team at Chandler."

"You should go out for tennis here," Harry said.

"Maybe next year," Sue replied, then picked up her purse. "Are we going now?"

"Yeah," I said, then mumbled, "let's get this over with."

"What'd you say?" Sue asked me.

"Nothing." I grabbed my paper cup of Coke and headed for the front of the restaurant.

Brian was too busy clowning around with everyone to notice us, but Ginger waved and gave us away. We were at the cashier by then, our backs to their booth, but I could feel Brian's stare piercing my back. Harry seemed to take forever to pay his bill: trying to find the exact change, then yielding to a ten dollar bill, finally arranging the singles he received as change before he moved out of the way. Whatever the cashier said, I didn't hear, as my ears were tuned to Brian's booth. I pocketed my change and headed for Sue and Harry, who were waiting by the entrance.

"Bye, hairy," Brian called in his distinctive mocking tone before we stepped outside. I wasn't going to let his insolence pass without a reply. Walking down the front sidewalk, I looked through the windows. Of his group, Brian was the only one still watching us, smirking. As we passed, I noticed his Camaro a few feet away. Without thinking of the consequences, I popped the lid on my cup of Coke and poured it on the shiny white hood. Then, afraid that Brian had seen, I began to walk faster, putting my hand against Sue's back and pushing her ahead.

"Come on," I whispered to her.

"What'd you do that for?" Sue asked, as I tried to hurry her along.

"Because he asked for it. Let's go."

"What's wrong?" Harry asked.

"Nothing." I tried the passenger's door, but it was locked. "Hurry up and unlock the door." I expected to see Brian sprint around the corner any moment. Finally, Harry flipped the lock and we got in.

"What do you want to do now?" Harry asked.

"Why don't we just drive?" I replied, anxious to leave the parking lot. As we turned past the restaurant, Brian was still visible through the front window. I had worried over nothing.

"How about Camelback Mountain?" Harry suggested by the time we reached Camelback Road. Before I could answer, he had turned right, heading toward the mountain. Northeast of downtown Phoenix, Camelback Mountain was more of a tall hill than a mountain; it resembled a camel's hump. From the top there was a great view of Phoenix and its desert suburbs, but no one went there for the view. It was a place I would have liked to go with Sue, but it was the last place I wanted to go with Sue and Harry.

"Why don't we just go home?" I told Harry. "I'm really tired."

We drove to Sue's house silently.

"I guess the best I can say about tonight is it's been interesting," Sue told me at her side door.

"I know what you mean," I said, wondering if she would let me kiss her. "I'm sorry things worked out this way. We won't do it like this again."

"Okay," she said, then added the magic words, "good night." It was time for our first kiss. But she turned quickly— too quickly for a kiss—and went in the house. Walking back to the car, I could only picture Rich and Patti giving each other hickeys. Life just wasn't being fair to me.

As Harry drove me home, I debated whether to thank him or not. Finally, I decided to say, "Thanks, Harry," with a slight sarcastic edge.

"That's okay, Allan. It was really a fun night. Sue's really nice."

"Yeah."

"We'll have to—"

"I'll see you Monday, Harry." I slammed the door and walked into the house. I didn't care if I cut the idiot off or not. He deserved to know what a jerk he was.

As I walked in, my mother was still dressed up from her evening out, emptying the dishwasher, her last chore before going to bed.

"How was your date?" she asked in all innocence.

I walked past her and started down the hall. "Awful. Just awful." Then I stopped and called back to her, "It would have been fine with a car, you know."

"I thought you understood why you couldn't have the car tonight," the Duke said, poking his head out their bedroom door.

"I didn't say it was your fault," I told him.

"That's good," the Duke said. "Because it's not."

I had to agree. It couldn't be their fault, because Harry was the one who had let me down. I should've known better than to rely on him.

I just hoped it hadn't ruined things with Sue.

Chapter Ten

SISTER SCHOOLS TIE

by Allan Antottle
Ocotillo Correspondent

Saturday morning, I forgot about Sue momentarily when I saw the High School Sports pages in the *Register*. There were only sixty-four words in my story, but the importance of each could not be diminished. This was Pulitzer Prize material.

Nothing escaped me, from the one typographical error (Ocotillo Stickehs for Ocotillo Stickers) in the first sentence to the omission of one line of statistics. No matter how small the story was, it seemed better than anything I had ever done for the *Observer*.

I was reading my story for the twentieth time that morning, when the phone rang around eleven o'clock. For some reason I got it in my head that Sue was calling to congratulate me.

"Hello?"

"Hi, Allan," the cute voice said.

"Oh, it's you," I said, sounding disappointed.

"Yes, it's me. I saw your story, I thought it was good, this is Sandy just in case you don't recognize my voice, I'll get off the phone now and leave you alone, bye."

"What?" I asked, half laughing at her one-breath performance. "Why're you hanging up?"

Then she said, "Because you always act like you don't want to talk to me."

She was right, but I wasn't going to admit it. "I do?"

"Like right now. In fact," she added, "it's too bad I don't want to be a dentist."

"Why?"

"Because I'm getting plenty of practice. I'm already an expert in pulling teeth."

"Okay, I get the message. It's just—"

"You don't have to tell me," she interrupted. "I don't think I want to hear. I'm sure you have your reasons. Teen correspondents are popular and very busy, and I just manage to get in the way."

"No, you don't," I told her.

"I don't?" she asked quickly, jumping on my careless remark.

"Well—"

"Forget it, Allan. I'll see you Monday."

"No, wait, Sandy," I said. I realized that "Sandy" had slipped off my tongue and out of my mouth without warning. What did I want to tell her? Fortunately, no one was around. "It's just that sometimes I have a lot on my mind, that's all. Sometimes you just say things in a funny way."

"I do?" she asked, intrigued by my confession. "Like what?"

"I can't think of any, but when I do, I'll tell you."

"But what about now? Are you just walking out the door?"

"No, I'm not walking out the door. I'm standing here with a bowl of raisin bran."

"Well, you didn't sound very happy to hear my voice."

"I thought you were someone else," I told her.

"Like who? Or don't you want to talk about it?"

"I thought you might be Sue Arnold."

"Oh," she said, backing right off.

"Only you're not." For some inexplicable reason, I decided to tell her: "We went out last night, only we didn't have the best time." I briefly described our three-person date. "Then we ran into someone I didn't want to see at Bob's Big Boy, but I'm trying not to think about that. So I know Sue had a bad time."

"I don't see how anyone could have a bad time with you," she said in that cute tone again.

"Now, see, right there," I said, getting animated, "that's what I don't like."

"What? What're you talking about?"

"What you just said: I don't see how anyone could have a bad time with you."

"What's wrong with saying that?"

"A lot. It sounds like—well, it sounds like you—I mean—"

"Spit it out, Allan. You're not making any sense."

How could I spell it out? Whenever she got that tone, she drove me crazy. She sounded sexy, cute, and—thin. She sounded like she was dying to go out with me. I just didn't want to think about pooling our genes.

"You know what I mean," I said.

"I don't know what you mean," she told me in an innocent voice.

"All right, I can't explain it."

"Then I'll change the subject. What else happened last night?" she asked. "With this mystery Someone. You're not talking about Brian Sawyer, are you?"

"What?" I was panicking. "How'd you know? Did someone tell you?" My armpits were beginning to drip. "Oh, great, it'll probably be all over school on Monday."

"Calm down, will you? He's not worth having a heart attack."

"But how'd you know it was him?"

"Anyone with brains could've figured it out," she told me. "Remember, I saw you with him at Cactus Drugs that night, and that one day in the cafeteria. I know how he acts. So what happened last night?"

I sighed and admitted the truth. "I gave Brian a reason to kill me."

"Why would you do a thing like that?"

"It's a long story."

"I have plenty of time, Allan, unless you don't want to tell me."

No one was home, but I wasn't sure I wanted to bare all my problems to Sandy.

"I don't know," I said. "I'd really like to stop thinking about it."

"Whatever you say," she said, sounding slightly hurt.

"I just don't want to talk about it."

"Fine," she said quickly.

Now I was feeling like a louse. I had every right not to tell her anything, but she made me feel as if I were cheating her out of the truth. I guess that's why I opened my mouth and told her what happened.

"You dumped a Coke on his car for saying goodbye to Harry?" she asked immediately. "What was he doing? Saying it sarcastically?"

Somehow, I couldn't tell her the rest of the story.

"He's always making fun of me and Harry. He thinks we're twins or something."

"Well, you've got to admit that it could look pretty funny being on a three-person date with Sue—and Harry."

"Well, it wasn't funny. And I don't know if Sue will ever go out with me again."

Sandy listened to my last statement carefully, then said, "I don't know if this'll help, but if she really likes you, she'll go out with you again."

"You think so?"

"I would," she said.

I had to change the subject. "I just don't want to talk about it any more," I said.

"Okay," she agreed. "It's your life. But if you ever change your mind, give me a call," she said, lightening her tone. "My number's in the book. Only I know you never will."

"How do you know that? Maybe I'll surprise you some-time," I said.

"I'd like that," she said eagerly.

"There, see, you did it again."

"Did what again?"

"You know, sounded funny—"

"I think you're going crazy, Allan."

I was laughing by then. I couldn't win with her, and I knew it. "I'm going to finish my soggy raisin bran. I'll see you Monday."

"Does this mean you're going to hang up?"

"Yes, I'm hanging up."

"At least you're in a better mood now, Mr. Correspon-dent."

She was right. I was, even if I had two unanswered questions pestering me: What in the world was I going to do about Brian? And why did it take a fat girl to cheer me up?

Chapter Eleven

Monday would be a day, I thought, for clearing up old business. Only the old business kept turning into new business.

Before school, I stopped by the j-room to see if the staffers had turned in any features for Friday's paper. I'd have to edit them before they went to the printer on Tuesday. I also wanted to know what the Comp thought of my *Register* story.

She was sitting in the back room, sipping a cup of coffee and reading the *Register*, when I walked in and popped the question.

"Yes, I saw it," she said. "I thought you wrote a very concise story. And that's what I want to talk about. What do you have in the paper this week?"

"Well, we're playing Los Gatos, so I'll be writing the story for that."

"I don't mean the *Register*. I mean the *Observer*."

"Oh, well—" Actually, I hadn't worked on anything all weekend. "I was going to finish up a story on the marching band. I have some other ideas, like a feature on the cast of the fall musical. But I'm still working on them."

"Allan, you know that a good writer can write about whatever's happening and make it relevant and interesting and important. You're very good at that. But I'd like you to write something deeper. Something that's a little less fluffy. Do you know what I mean?"

"Well, yeah, no more marching-band stories," I said. "Right? Only it's hard to find stories like that every week."

"I don't care about every week," she said. "I just want a few this year. We have a reputation to uphold. Remember Sara Ingersoll?"

I nodded. How could I forget Sara Ingersoll? The Comp mentioned her so often that I thought she was a saint. She had been feature editor the year I was a freshman. Compton idolized her for writing a series of stories on the conditions in the state juvenile detention homes, the most notorious of which was Fort Grant.

"Her series on Fort Grant is more what I'm after here. Why don't you reread that and see what ideas you can come up with?"

"I'll see what I can do," I assured her. But I wasn't sure that I wanted to follow in Sara Ingersoll's footsteps. After all, she had graduated and gone to Maricopa Community College. The last I heard was that she had taken a part-time job writing obituaries for the *Phoenix Gazette*—not exactly the big-time career I had in mind.

"Think positively," Compton continued, "you *will* find a blockbuster, maybe even for next week. Right?"

I nodded. As I started to check my in basket, I had to agree. Writing a blockbuster would only improve my reputation.

"Allan!"

Vicky Lincoln had walked into the back room. Now she was shoving a piece of paper at me.

"Read this," she said, flapping the page against my nose.

"What is it?"

"Just part of my column," she said.

I took the paper and read the short typewritten paragraph:

The Observing Eye hears that a new monarch (a for-mer-frog-turned-prince) has just established his own re-public. The question is: is there a princess named Sue in his life? A new republic needs a couple this cute.

I blushed, but not from pain.

"You're not really going to put this in your column?"

"You've hit the big time, kiddo."

With that, my ego inflated to twice its usual size.

"But where'd you find out about Sue?"

"I never reveal my sources," Vicky said.

"I bet it was Ginger. She saw us at Bob's on Friday night."

Vicky shrugged mysteriously, while I scanned the paragraph again.

"Do you think you could drop that frog part and just use my initials or something? She might not understand that it's about us. That way she'd definitely understand."

"That'd take all the fun out of it, Allan. She'll get it, some-how." Then she leaned against me and whispered, "I'll tell her what it means."

"You will?" She nodded. Then I realized what that meant. Vicky might tell more about me and my past than I wanted. "No, that's okay," I said. "I'll handle it. I'll tell her it's about us."

"Whatever you say," Vicky said.

Then I, a newly crowned prince waiting for his princess, was ready to tackle his next order of business for the day. I skipped first-hour P.E. and went to the Office.

"What do you need?" the registrar's secretary asked. She was a real automaton.

"I want to switch P.E."

"Did your counselor approve it?"

I could see the red tape beginning to tangle. I headed for the counselors' offices, which were right around the corner. I was going to change P.E., even if I was late for second-hour Chemistry.

"You'll need to see Miss Pampreen," the secretary at the Counseling Center said, "but she's with someone now. Why don't you have a seat?"

As I turned and headed for the chairs that lined the far wall, I saw Sandra Parker sitting there, looking like a fat lump.

"Hi, Allan," she said. "What are you doing here?"

"Cutting class," I said, as I sat two chairs away.

"No, really, what're you doing?"

Why couldn't she just leave me alone? It was one thing to talk to her on the phone and hear her sexy voice and tell her some personal stuff, but it was a whole other story to see her in person. What if someone saw us talking as if we liked each other? "I need to talk to Pampreen," I muttered.

"I have to see Underhill. I need some information about the PSAT."

I was surprised. Somehow, I figured Sandra would get married, have six kids and watch soap operas all day. "Oh, I should do that, too."

"Where're you going to college?" she asked.

I shrugged. "I don't know. Someone told me I should go to college in New York City."

"That's too bad."

"Why?" I asked. "What's wrong with New York?"

"Because I'm going to be in California. I'm going to try to get into Stanford. Either that or UCLA. They both have good political science programs."

"All I know is I want to go somewhere to major in journalism."

"Is that what you're seeing Pampreen about?" She was certainly persistent.

I sighed and gave up. "No, I just need to switch a class."

"Not English, I hope," she said.

"P.E."

"What's wrong with P.E.?"

At that moment, a student left and the secretary told me I could see Miss Pampreen.

"It's about Brian," I whispered to Sandra.

"Good luck," Sandra called, as I escaped from her clutches.

As I entered her office, Miss Pampreen was propped against the wall in her desk chair, hands resting on her head. She looked as if she was keeping the wall from falling.

"What can I do for you, Allan?" she asked pleasantly enough, retracting her pose.

"Would it be possible, I mean, I want to change P.E. classes," I said forthrightly. "I have Coach MacAddino and I'd like to change."

She studied my face for a moment. "What's your rationale behind this?" she asked and turned away.

"It's kind of hard to explain," I said. She was staring out her window, not saying a word. "There's this kid who gives me a hard time," I tried. "He did it all last year, and I thought maybe he'd forget—over the summer, you know—but he didn't. He's in P.E. with me, and I can't stand it anymore."

"Who's this other boy?"

I bowed my head and hoped it would end soon. "Brian Sawyer."

"And how does he tease you?"

"Well, he doesn't really tease me," I said, inspecting my fingernails. "He just calls me names. Okay?"

"What does he call you?" I looked up and found her watching me. "What names does he call you?" she repeated.

My face began to burn. "You don't understand. It's not going to sound bad to you. I just, no, I—"

"Don't be afraid to level with me. I've heard it all. I'll understand. It's my job. I was a coach for fifteen years. And I can't help you until I know the full story."

Sanctuary was just one word away. I had to force myself.

"All right," I said, then swallowed and looked at the picture of the stallion on the wall behind her. "He calls me 'hairy.'"

She started to look at my folder on her desk. "But your name is Allan—"

"No, not that, not the name, the—"

"Ooooh," she moaned appreciatively, "I see." She nodded slowly. "Well, let's see what we can do."

But there was nothing to be done. Even with her approval, I couldn't change P.E., because all the other junior P.E. sections conflicted with classes I was taking.

"You could always take him off the school grounds and teach him a lesson. You're obviously more of a man than he is," she told me.

I think my mouth dropped about two miles. "Do you know who Brian Sawyer is?" I rejoined. "He'd tear me into a million pieces."

I left her office feeling helpless. At least first period was over now, and I had managed to avoid Brian for another day. If I could only find a reason to miss P.E. the rest of the year, I'd be all set.

Since I had chemistry next, I started down the breezeway toward the science building, when I saw Paul Everson, a staffer on the paper, walking toward me.

"Hi, Allan," he said.

"Hi, Paul," I said, and continued on my way.

Suddenly, I was pushed up against a row of lockers.

"Where were you this morning, you little chicken?"

I tried to laugh, hoping that it was a joke, but Brian pushed his forearm harder against my throat.

"You could've ruined the finish on my car, creep."

I tried to adjust my position to keep my throat from hurting.

"You understand what I'm telling you?"

I quickly focused on his face to make sure he wanted an answer, then glanced away just as quickly. I nodded.

A couple of guys from P.E. walked by then and saw us.

"Hey, Sawyer, leave him alone," one of them said.

But Brian was unperturbed.

"You don't do stuff like that to me," he said, snarling in my face. Then he kneed me and walked away.

I went down on my knees, but my only thought was to act as

if nothing bad happened, even as I was reeling in pain and fearing the worst.

I WAS A TEENAGE EUNUCH!
Savage Attack Turns Boy to Babe

I pretended that I had dropped some papers and began leafing through my notebook.

"What're you doing?" someone asked me.

I looked up and saw Rich standing there, flanked by Brad and a few other JV jocks.

"Nothing," I said, ignoring the pain. I continued to rifle through my notebook. "I'm just looking for something, that's all."

"Sitting on the breezeway?" he asked. "What did Sawyer do to you, anyway?"

Everyone walking by now was staring at me as if something was wrong.

"Nothing," I said and tried to stand up. But the pain in my groin made me double over.

"Hey, Rich, there's Patti and Diane," Brad told him.

"Let's find out what they're doing tonight," Rich told him. "Maybe they'll go over to Austin's." Brad and the others headed for the girls, but Rich looked down at me. "Don't be late for class," he joked.

I forced a smile and nodded quickly. "Yeah, yeah," I said, and he walked away.

Then, when the pain had almost subsided a few moments later, I stood up and headed for class. By the time I walked into chemistry, my eyes had stopped watering. And by the time it was over, I felt (almost) normal again.

Through it all, I had learned one lesson: I would never be able to avoid Brian. Somehow I was going to have to face him.

Chapter Twelve

Did you see my story Saturday?" I asked C.J. in homeroom later that morning.

"What story?" he had the nerve to ask.

"In the *Register*."

"I was in L.A. Remember?"

"I didn't forget," I told him. "I just thought maybe you saw Saturday's paper when you got home."

"I was too busy recuperating," he said.

"That's nice," I said halfheartedly.

"I think the *Register* needs a new typesetter, though."

"What?"

"Of course, I saw your story. Complete with typo," he told me, smiling. "How could I not read your story? But next week, how about two paragraphs?"

"My sentiments exactly," I replied, relieved that he had paid attention to my story. "So what did you do in L.A.?"

"So much I can't even remember. You know, shopping in Beverly Hills, getting stuck on the freeways, a really fancy dinner at Le Dôme. How was your weekend?" he asked then.

"Not as exciting as yours." I had decided not to mention my date with Sue, or my problem with Brian. "The usual stuff."

"A story in the *Register* isn't usual stuff."

"Yeah, that's right," I said, pleased that he was reminding me.

"The glories of fame."

"Well, it's not all that it's cracked up to be. Compton saw my story, and now she wants me to write bigger and better stories for the *Observer*. I think she's jealous that I'm writing for the *Register*. She says she wants blockbusters from me."

"What kind of blockbusters?" C.J. asked.

"I think she wants me to be Geraldo Rivera or something. Only I can't think of anything."

"You'll think of something," C.J. said.

"Or die trying," I added. "Maybe we can come up with something at lunch. Or are you eating here today?" C.J. went on more errands at lunch than anyone I ever knew.

He smiled.

"I know. Don't tell me," I said. "Errands."

"Perceptive," he said.

As we walked from homeroom to English, I saw Sue standing in the hall talking to a girl I didn't know.

"See you in English," I told C.J. and darted toward Sue.

"Hi," I said, interrupting their conversation.

"Oh, hi," Sue replied.

"See you later," the girl told Sue and left.

"Where're you going?" I asked her.

"English," she said.

"With who?"

"Vorhees."

Mrs. Vorhees taught regular junior English. "I'm going to Briggs's English class. I'll walk you." She started down the hall with me, without saying anything.

I decided to take advantage of our chance meeting.

"I wanted to ask you out for Friday. We won't double this time. I mean, I can get the car," I was telling her before I gave her a chance to reply. "I still have to sit in the press box, but after the game I'll write my story there, too, so you can come up and be with me. Does that sound okay?"

"That sounds nice," she said, as we stopped in front of Vorhees's class, "but I don't think so."

I looked at her, not totally understanding. "You mean—"

"I can't really go out with you this week."

"You can't?"

She shook her head.

"What about next week? It's Homecoming, you know."

"Ask me then," was all she said, and she went into class.

I must've looked like my world had ended as I walked into English.

"What's wrong with you?" Sandy asked.

"Why?" I practically barked, as I sat at my desk.

"You don't look like you're in a very good mood, that's all."

I glanced at C.J. What if he began to wonder how Sandy knew what my moods were?

"I'm not," I said, keeping my back to her. "It's been a lousy day."

"You want to talk about it?" she asked.

I shook my head. I wasn't going to carry on a conversation with her in English, where everyone could see. But after the bell rang and Briggs started discussing Hawthorne's symbolism, she slipped me a note.

It read:

Allan,
I'm worried about you. Did everything go okay with Pampreen?

                                                                Sandy

I nodded slightly. Then she pushed another piece of paper into my ribs. It read:

I wonder where my pliers are? I may have to start pulling teeth again.

I turned around quickly and grimaced at her. This wasn't the time or the place for us to have a conversation or pass notes.

"Is there a problem, Allan?"

Briggs had nailed me.

"Nuh—no!" I protested. I saw C.J. turn to look at me, and I continued, stuttering like a fool, "N-no problem."

"You can talk to Sandy after class," Briggs announced to everyone.

Humiliated, I shifted my eyes to the graffiti carved into my desk and found an appropriate sentiment: BRIGGS STINKS.

By that time, Briggs had returned to Hawthorne, and I was deciding how I would explain what happened if C.J. asked. A moment later, I felt Sandy's finger jab me in the side, as if to say that I deserved what had happened.

This time I didn't turn around.

After History, C.J. took off for his errands, and I headed for lunch. I saw Harry walk into the cafeteria, so I sat on the patio to avoid him. But I wasn't in the mood for lunch the more I thought about Sue. I wondered if I should confront her in Spanish and demand to know if she wanted to go out with me again. I stuffed half of my sandwich back into my lunch bag and got up. I needed to get away from everyone to think about my predicament.

Since it was lunchtime, the breezeways were empty, and I figured I could have twenty minutes of peace to collect my thoughts before Spanish began. That's when I saw C.J., sitting in the grassy alley between the Social Science Building and the Language Building.

"What're you doing here?" I called to him. He looked up, surprised. "I thought you had some errands or something."

"Oh, I did," he said, as I walked over to him. "But I got them over with, and I just needed some time alone. It's such a zoo in that cafeteria. Most of those kids are such pigs."

"What'd you do, stop at Taco Bell or something?" I asked, sitting beside him. Taco Bell was the closest fast-food joint to the school.

"Oh, yeah," he said. "How come you're here? You can't be *that* anxious to get to Spanish."

"I just didn't feel like eating," I reported. "Actually, my lunch was fine," I told him, swatting at my brown-paper bag. "The problem's more complicated."

He took my lunch bag and peered inside. "So what happened?" he asked, as he helped himself to the Oreos. He noticed I was staring at him then and quickly asked, "You didn't want these, did you? You said you weren't hungry."

"No, I don't want them," I said. "Harry and I doubled on Friday," I explained. "And it didn't work out."

"I thought you weren't friends with him," he said. "So why'd you double with him, then?"

"It's a long story...." My voice trailed off. I wasn't going to tell C.J.

"Oh, I get it," he said. "You needed someone to go with when I wouldn't. Right? Someone to drive, I bet."

"Kind of," I admitted.

"Harry drove, didn't he?"

"Yeah, but that wasn't the problem. It was just Sue and me and Harry, and Sue got stuck with him during the game, because I had to be in the press box."

"Sounds like fun," he said. "Do you want this?" he asked, retrieving the other half of my sandwich from the lunch sack.

"I thought you ate lunch."

"I'm just a growing boy."

I shrugged as he took a large bite. I continued, "If my parents would've just let me use the car. Or buy me one—like you. You're so lucky that your parents bought you your own car."

"Yeah," he said, and finished the sandwich. Then he looked at me and said, "You know, Allan, I've been thinking about you. I think I have a blockbuster story idea for you."

"Yeah?" I was skeptical, but intrigued.

"How about an exposé of the Party House?" he said.

"Oh, sure, right. I don't even know where the place is."

"But I do," he said and grinned.

"*You* do?" He may have been unconventional, but he hardly seemed the party type. "You've been there before?"

"A few times. So why don't we go on Saturday? I'll pick you up at eight."

"The Party House," I said, half aloud, thinking about the story possibilities. I could see page one of the *Register* now:

TEEN DRUG AND SEX DEN EXPOSED!
Ocotillo Correspondent Risks Life
to Close Down Illegal Party House

"I know," I said, scaling down my idea a little. "I could do 'A Night at the Party House.' Just report what I see, what's happening there, the type of kids. Maybe I could even get a two or three-part series out of it. That'd really show Compton," I said.

"Oh, say, before I forget, I forgot my gas credit cards today, and my car's almost out of gas. Can you loan me ten bucks?"

"Oh, well—" I knew I was sounding hesitant, but I was trying to remember exactly how much money I had.

"I'll pay you back tomorrow, if you're worried."

"I'm not worried," I said. I pulled out my wallet and took out ten one-dollar bills, the better part of my allowance for the week.

"I'll pay you back," he reassured me. I normally wouldn't have thought twice about lending money to someone like C.J., except for the fact that he kept saying he would pay me back. I don't know why exactly, but I wasn't sure I believed him.

"So where's the Party House?" I asked, as he tucked the money into his jeans. I was dying to know.

"Off Camelback Road," he said. "I'll take you there Saturday night."

"Why don't we go somewhere after school?" I suggested. "Now that you've got gas money, you can drive and I'll buy. Wherever you want. We could go to—"

"I'll see you later," he said suddenly, standing up and brushing off his pants.

"Where're you going? The bell's not going to ring yet."

"Things to do, places to go. See you tomorrow," he said, then waved and walked away.

Had I said something wrong? Maybe he thought I only wanted to be friends because he had his own car. But I had only asked him to drive once. That couldn't be it. Maybe he just had something on his mind. And why was he sitting between the buildings anyway? He hadn't had time to go anywhere and eat lunch, too. Something wasn't right.

I just didn't know what it was.

But I didn't think much more about it that afternoon. As soon as I walked into journalism class, Vicky Lincoln beckoned me with her index finger.

"I changed your story," she said. "I'm just finishing it now."

"Did you get rid of the frog part?" I asked, walking to her desk.

"Well, not exactly. You'll see." She handed me a sheet from a yellow legal pad.

ANIMAL NEWS
(a play in two acts)

Act 1: Friday night, Bob's Big Boy. Frog Eyes gives Thumb to Big B.
Act 2: Monday morning, OHS. Big B. gives Knee to Frog Eyes. Better watch out, Froggie!
Will there be an Act 3? Stay tuned.

"You're not going to put that in, are you?" I said, wanting to crumple the paper.

"Well, of course. It's perfect for my column. It's kind of cute, don't you think?"

"But what about the other one?" I asked. "I thought you were going to use it."

"You were right," she said. "It was too hard to understand. This one's better. It has more action. This is definitely big-time stuff, kiddo."

I could've thought of a million other ways to hit the big time than this one, but I knew it wouldn't do any good to beg. I smiled, because I didn't know what else to do, said something dumb, then went into the classroom to work.

Chapter Thirteen

That night I sulked through dinner. Everyone was a problem: Harry, then Sue, Brian, now Vicky. So after dinner I decided to call C.J., just to talk. Maybe he'd have some helpful ideas. I looked up Blankenship in the phone book. There were four numbers, but I dialed the only one that fell within Ocotillo's district.

A man answered.

"Can I talk to C.J.?" I asked.

"Who is this?" the man wanted to know.

I didn't like his tone. "Allan," I said, starting to feel nervous. "I'm a friend of his."

"Well, he's not here."

"Will he be back soon?" I asked. "Could I leave a message?"

"He doesn't live here anymore."

"Oh," I said, but I forged on in my best reporter style, as if I weren't the least bit surprised. "Can you tell me where he does live so I can call him?"

"You'll have to ask him that," the man said, then hung up the phone.

I wasn't sure what all this meant, but I saw a new C.J. emerging:

MYSTERIOUS PHONE CALL
EXPOSES TROUBLED TEEN

I tried the other Blankenships in the phone book, just in case C.J. was there, but no one else knew who he was. I was beginning to wonder if I knew him myself.

I stalled for a while then, postponing making any decisions. Then I did the only thing I could think of doing. And, as I dialed the phone (in my parents' bedroom, for privacy), I hoped I wouldn't regret it.

"Hi."

"Hi."

"Is that all you have to say?" I asked.

"I thought the caller was supposed to say something."

"Don't you know who this is?"

"If I thought you were some heavy breather, Allan, I would've hung up on you by now." Sandy was sounding just as cute as ever in her telephone voice.

"All right. Are you busy?"

"I'm not eating raisin bran, if that's what you mean. Actually, I just finished the dishes. And I only have *The Scarlet Letter* to look forward to tonight. Is everything okay? You seemed upset today."

"I got in another fight with Brian."

"When?"

"After I saw you in the Counseling Center. He ambushed me after I left the office, and kneed me."

"What?" she asked.

"You know." I wasn't going to spell it out.

"God. Are you all right?"

"Yeah, I'm fine."

"I don't understand what's going on between the two of you, so if you don't mind my asking, why did you dump the Coke?

I know you said it was a long story, but if you told me, maybe I could help."

At that point, I was willing to try anything. "I told you he said, 'Bye, hairy.' Only he wasn't talking to Harry," I explained. "He was talking about me."

"I don't understand. You said that he said—"

I interrupted before she could go any further: "Hairy Harry, hairy Allan."

"Harry Allan? Oh, hairy Allan. Hairy Allan? *Hairy* Allan?"

"That's what he meant. He said it to make me mad, not Harry."

"Are you?" she asked in that cute tone of hers.

"What?" I asked, playing dumb.

"You know. Hairy." She paused, then repeated, "Are you?"

"It's not funny," I told her.

"No, Allan, come on," she said, getting even cuter, "are you? I won't tell anyone."

"There's nobody left to tell."

"Then you are. Where?"

I summoned my courage and said, "My chest." She was silent for so long that I had to ask, "Are you there?"

"That's sexy," she said finally.

"Sandy—"

"You're not blushing, are you?"

I could feel my face burning. "Nuh—no," I stammered.

"Well, I don't care what Brian thinks, I think it's cute."

"That's you and no one else."

"Doesn't Sue think it's sexy?" she asked.

"We only had one date," I reminded her. "And Harry was there. Remember?"

"Well, someday, you'll meet a girl who'll appreciate it."

"Yeah, if I don't kill myself first," I said. "The worst part is that someone told Vicky about our fight, and she's putting it in her column for Friday."

"Poor Allan," she teased. "And I bet Sue won't go out with you, either."

"How'd you know?"

"Because it's just your luck, isn't it?"

"Well, yeah," I said. "Things never seem to work out the way I want."

"Oh, you mean, you never wanted to be feature editor or teen correspondent?"

"No, I mean, they never work out exactly the way—oh, you know what I mean."

"Can I tell you something?" she asked. "Can I be honest with you?"

I was afraid to say yes.

"Well?" she asked.

"I guess."

"You caused your own problem with Brian Friday night. He said two words: 'Bye, hairy.' Or maybe he said: 'Bye, Harry.' You really don't know for sure. But even if he was talking about you, you went ahead and started World War III. For what? *Two* words. Pardon me, Allan, but I hope you never become president. Although, I have to admit, I'd vote for you if you were on the ballot."

"But—" I wanted to argue about all the things that Brian had done to me, but she cut me off.

"Look at it from Brian's point of view," she continued. "He's with some friends, being his dumb-jock self, and a punk walks by and messes with his car. What do you think he's going to do? Say thank you? Give you a big bouquet?"

"No, I—"

"If you would leave him alone, he would have to leave you alone, too."

That stopped me cold. "You think so? Really?"

"Look, you started it with the Coke routine. Now he's gotten revenge, so you're starting from scratch. Just let him alone this time—no matter what he does to provoke you. He can't beat you up every day. He just wants to get under your skin, and you do a good job of letting him. Why don't you stop it now?"

I had to agree with her, even if I still wanted revenge.

"Are you sure you're not going to be a preacher or something?" I asked.

She laughed. "I get carried away sometimes," she said "That's why I want to go into politics."

"Maybe *you'll* run for president," I told her.

"I hardly think so," she said, sounding annoyed. Then knew why: any woman would have a hard enough time bein elected president, without being fat as well. "I'd rather worl behind the scenes," she added. Then she said, "I should rea some more Hawthorne. Just lighten up a little."

She sounded as if she really cared.

Wednesday morning, Brian ribbeted or "hair-Harryed" a me every chance he got. At first, I was angry, but I reminde myself that anger wouldn't help, so I calmed down and staye that way. Every time Brian ribbeted, I pretended that I hadn heard. Instead, I imagined that I was subjecting him to Chines water torture. After a while, he seemed to forget about me. O so I thought.

Near the end of the period, as I was hurrying down a nar row row of lockers on my way to the showers, blind without m contact lenses, I started to walk around someone who wa moving too slowly for my pace. It was only when I was inche away that I realized I had begun to pass the wrong person Brian.

He froze immediately, blocking my way with his arm "Going somewhere?" he asked.

For once, I wasn't going to let myself be intimidated. I foun myself saying, "I'm going to the showers. Would you move ou of the way, please?"

"'Please?'" he mimicked. "What kind of wimp are you Make me, hairy."

I sighed. I had been through this so many times with him tha it was easier to ignore his anger now. It was also easier becaus half the class was crowded around us, waiting to see wha would happen. "Aren't you tired of that same old line?" asked.

"What's the matter, hairy?" he taunted, yanking a tuft o hair on my chest.

I flinched slightly, but I persisted. "Why are you so fascinated by my chest hair? You want some for your own?" His chest was as broad and as bare as the Mojave Desert.

I could tell he was thinking about pounding me, and nothing I could do would stop him.

"Sawyer's a queer," an anonymous voice called out from the crowd. If I had been a ventriloquist, I couldn't have planned it better.

"I am not!" Brian protested immediately. Someone had found Brian's number.

I stared defiantly at Brian.

"Hey, Sawyer," someone behind me yelled, "move it."

"We're going to be late," another guy called.

"Sawyer, you jerk!" someone else yelled.

Then someone in the rear started shoving, and the momentum carried us all past Brian. He just stood there, unable to say a word.

"You look like you're feeling better than yesterday," Sandy said when she saw me walk into English. Then she winked at me, as if we shared a secret.

"Much better," I said. After our phone call last night, it wasn't as hard to look at her as I thought it would be. "I think Brian's going to leave me alone."

"What happened?" she asked anxiously. "Tell me."

"I'll tell you later," I said, looking in the direction of C.J.'s desk. He hadn't been in homeroom and now he wasn't in English, and I had a lot of questions for him. "Have you seen C.J. today?" I asked her.

She shook her head. "Why?"

"I needed to ask him something, that's all."

"Is something wrong?" she asked.

I thought about my mysterious phone call and our supposed visit to the Party House.

"I wish I knew," I told her, before Briggs called the class to order.

* * *

Wednesday night Sandy called me.

"Our phone calls are getting to be a habit," she announced. "Do you think we'll go blind?"

I groaned. "Did you finish the dishes?"

"Of course," she said. "Have you finished your raisin bran?"

"No, I'm on my third bowl tonight."

She asked about Brian then, but nothing new had happened. In fact, I was worried more about what had happened to C.J. than any retaliation from Brian.

C.J. hadn't been in school for two days, and I wanted to know why. For one thing, I was worried about him, but I was also getting worried about our visit to the Party House Saturday night. What if he forgot? I'd never find a better story to make the Comp happy.

"I'm worried about C.J.," I told her. "He hasn't been in school since Monday, and I think something's wrong." I told her about my strange phone call. "If he doesn't come back to school tomorrow, can you check in the office and find out where he lives? I don't know what else to do."

"Well, I'm not supposed to look at student records," Sandy said, "but I could probably find out if I wanted. What do you think's wrong?"

"I don't know. Maybe he got kicked out of the house. Maybe he's in some kind of trouble. I don't know. But whoever I talked to was really weird."

"I'll check it out," Sandy volunteered.

"I knew I could count on you," I said.

"How high can you count?" she teased, sounding like Mae West.

I started to laugh, but I wasn't sure I understood her joke. Was she referring to her weight? Or her body?

"Well?" she prompted.

"What?" I was stalling.

"Aren't you going to answer my question?"

"What question?"

"Oh, Allan, you're no fun. You're supposed to be Cary Grant to my Mae West."

"What?"

"You're supposed to say something charming and witty—and, well, *sexxxx-y*," she said.

I took a slow breath.

"Okay," I said, keeping a straight face. "'Something charming and witty.'"

I thought she would groan then, or change the subject.

"And?" she asked. I was confused. "Finish your statement. And *what*?"

"What do you mean?" I asked.

"Something charming and witty and—what was the other word I used?"

I felt completely trapped. Why couldn't I say "sexy" and get it over with?

"Cat got your tongue?" she teased.

"What could a cat do with my tongue?" I joked, trying to get her off the subject. "On second thought, don't answer that."

We laughed, but changed the subject.

Chapter Fourteen

Sandy could have begun a detective agency. Thursday morning, she gave me two phone numbers for C.J. The first was the one I had called; that number had been deleted on C.J.'s record. The second number was the new number, and it belonged to his aunt. I realized immediately that C.J. was living with Aunt Faye.

When I tried to call his aunt's number during lunch, the strangest thing happened.

"The number you have dialed," the prerecorded voice of some long-dead operator told me, "has been disconnected." I waited, thinking I might be told what the new number was. "The number you have dialed has been disconnected," the voice repeated. Then I heard a beep and a live operator asked, "What number were you calling?"

When I told her, she reiterated that the number had been disconnected.

"But isn't there a new number?"

"No, and thank you for using Mountain Bell."

"But—"

She disconnected me.

I must have tried to call the number a hundred times on Thursday and Friday, but every time I heard the same voice.

I was no closer to finding C.J. than I had been before.

Friday night, as I took my seat at the breakfast bar for a fast hamburger supper, Rich asked me for a ride to the game.

I didn't react right away.

"Allan," Rich said, waving a hand in front of my eyes. "A ride?"

"I guess it doesn't matter now. I don't have a date."

"What happened to Sue?" Rich asked. "Did she stand you up or something?"

"No, she didn't stand me up. She just had other plans."

I wasn't in the mood to discuss Sue any further, especially with Rich.

"Are you going with Harry Snyder?" he asked. "Aren't you two still friends?"

I shrugged, trying to forget about Harry as well as Rich. But Rich kept plugging away.

"That was great how he made the tennis team."

My mind summoned up the headline that had surprised me in the *Observer* that day:

JUNIOR MAKES VARSITY TENNIS IN PERFECT FIRST ATTEMPT
High Hopes for Neophyte Netman

Thanks to Vicky's column, I was still Frog Eyes (even if I was a contact-wearing feature editor and teen correspondent who wrote the marching band story on page three), but Harry was going to be a Net Star. Maybe he'd trip and fall over the net.

"No, I'm not going with Harry. Why would I go anywhere with him?"

"What'd he do? Dump you for a friend?"

That was the last straw. "Do you want a ride or not?" I warned.

"Can't you take a joke?" Rich asked.

"Yeah, if it's a joke. Come on, I'm leaving in twenty minutes," I told him. "You don't need a ride home, do you?"

"No, I'm going over to Brad's with Patti," he said. "They can give me a ride."

That night, I may have been a big-shot reporter, but I was lonely without a date.

The first half had just ended, and I was deciding what I wanted to do during halftime, when Sandy walked into the press box. I hate to admit it now, but I imagined, as she walked toward me in her down jacket, that I was going to be mauled by a mauve polar bear.

"I have something to ask you," she said right away.

"I should do some things," I said, indicating my stat books.

"I know," she said. "You're busy. I'll leave in a minute. First I want to know if you're here with anyone tonight."

"You know the answer to that." I wasn't sure what she was up to now.

"Why don't we go somewhere and get something to eat? My treat."

"I have to finish the game," I told her.

"Not now, silly," she said. "Afterward."

I mulled over her suggestion. I was lonely, and I wouldn't mind some company. But I didn't want to go anywhere public. "Okay, if I can pick the place."

"Sure." She sounded a little surprised. "I guess I could let a celebrity choose his favorite spot."

"I wouldn't call myself a celebrity," I said.

"Well, you made Vicky's column, didn't you?" she told me. "Actually, I didn't think it was that bad. I don't think most kids will understand what she's talking about."

"I guess. The problem is that *I* know."

"Look, Allan, do you really care? You used to wear glasses, now you don't. You look great in your contacts. You did one dumb thing with Brian, and it's printed in the paper. So what? What's the big deal? You're letting it get to you the way you let Brian get to you."

"How would you like to be plastered all over the paper?"

"I wouldn't call two sentences being plastered all over the paper," Sandy argued.

"Why do you care so much? You're almost yelling at me," I told her.

"Because I'm really tired of the way you carry on about all of this stuff. And if you want my advice, you wouldn't let them bother you. I've heard what they say about me. Parker the Pig. Pork Chop Parker." I winced at her bluntness. "They can say what they want, it doesn't bother me. Their small minds have a hard time keeping busy."

"You really don't care?"

"Not what *they* say," she said. "Maybe what *someone else* says, but not them."

I wasn't sure what she meant, so I said nothing.

"Where should we meet?" she asked before she headed for the door.

"Why don't I meet you in front of the gym? I'll probably be twenty minutes late or so. You know, my story. I have to write it and phone it in."

"How could I forget that?" she asked. "That's all you ever talk about. Anyway, for you I can wait that long," she teased.

I wrote my story in a quiet corner of the locker room, then phoned the *Register*'s sports desk. By the time I left, most people had gone home. The parking lot was almost empty, except for the cars of a few players and the coaches. Sandra was standing in front of the gym, waiting patiently for me.

"Who's driving?" she asked.

"I have another idea," I said. "Why don't we walk somewhere? Let me throw my notebooks in my car," I continued, not giving her a chance to protest, "and I'll be right back."

As I walked in the direction of my car, I suddenly realized that it was no longer there. I mentally retraced my route to school that night, finishing with my arrival in the parking lot. I had parked *there* and my car *was* missing.

"I can't find my car," I told her, as I walked back to the front of the gym. "It's not there."

"Are you sure?"

"Of course, I'm sure. It's not there."

"Do you think someone stole it?"

"I don't know," I said. "I guess."

A moment later, as I was deciding whether to call the Duke, I saw two pairs of headlights turn into the parking lot. The cars raced across the lot and finally stopped in front of the gym. One of them was my car.

Then the door opened, and Rich and Patti got out. When Rich saw me, standing a short distance away, he started walking toward me, grinning like a lobotomized monkey, jangling a set of keys.

"Sorry I'm late," he said. "I thought the game would be longer. You won't say anything, will you?"

If a policeman had been beside me, I would've turned him in without a second thought. I was furious. He had no right to take the car.

"You won't say anything, right?" he repeated.

I glared at him.

Then the driver of the other car honked the horn. I glanced and saw Brad through the windshield.

"Go on and get in the car," he told Patti, then walked over to me.

"Why'd you take the car?" I demanded, when she had slammed the door.

"I had to pick Patti up from work," he explained. "I was careful."

"Do you know what would've happened if a cop stopped you? You wouldn't be able to get your license till you're twenty-one."

"No cop's going to stop me. I look like I'm sixteen."

I tried another approach. "Where'd you get the keys?" I asked, pointing to the key chain in his hand.

"I had them made. I just took Mom's keys one day and had them copied."

"Let me see," I said, and he handed them to me. Then without warning, I lobbed them as far as I could in the direction of the irrigation ditch.

He seemed unperturbed. "I can get another set made. Anyway, I don't even need the keys. Brad knows how to hot-wire a car."

"You're going to do this again?"

"I've done it lots of times. You just don't know."

"If you take it once more, I'm going to tell Mom and Dad."

"Look, I'm careful," he said, turning on the charm. "You really wouldn't say anything to Mom and Dad, would you? I'm not hurting anyone."

"Why didn't you just have Brad take you to pick up Patti?"

He grinned. "More fun this way. You won't say anything, right?"

I was angry, but part of me admired his guts. "Look, Rich. This is the second thing you've asked me not to tell. What're you going to ask me next time?"

He started toward Brad's car. "I won't ask you for any more favors," he said. "I promise."

"Yeah, sure."

He opened the door and slid in after Patti. Just as he slammed the door shut, I heard Brad make a sound that made me cringe.

He oinked. Twice.

Then they were gone.

"Sorry about that," I told Sandy, meaning the oinks. "They're asking for trouble."

But Sandy ignored my apology.

"Where are we going?" she asked.

"Well, why don't we walk to the 7-Eleven and get something there?" That would take us across the dark intramural fields and half a mile down a dark subdivision road. No one would ever spot us.

"Are you sure you don't want to drive somewhere?" she asked.

"Walking is more fun. Anyway, it'll do you—us, I mean—good to walk," I told her, as I started for the playing fields.

"What do you mean by that?" she asked, running after me. I could hear her down jacket swishing behind me.

"Nuh—nothing," I said. I would have to watch what I said about her weight.

"Are you sure you don't want to change your mind? It might be dangerous."

"Why?"

"Because no one'll see what we're doing out here," she said, as we left the last security light behind. I hadn't thought of it that way. Then she giggled. "Boy, is it dark!"

"And what do *you* mean by that?" I asked, beginning to feel nervous.

"Nothing. It's just your dirty mind." She waited for me to answer, but I just kept walking. "I'm kidding, you know."

"I know," I said.

"Well, you were being quiet. I thought you took it the wrong way."

"I don't take anything the wrong way," I boasted.

"Well, I'm glad that's cleared up," she said, and laughed. "I meant to tell you that I saw your story today on the marching band. That was more memorable than Vicky's column."

"Yeah, my story was a real masterpiece, right? Just wait till next week. I have a real blockbuster planned."

"What is it?"

"I don't know if I should talk about it," I told her. "But I guess I could tell you." I couldn't resist sharing my information with someone. "I'm going to do an exposé on the Party House. At least I think I am. C.J.'s supposed to take me there tomorrow night. If he ever appears again. You know, that number was disconnected."

"I know," she said, "you keep telling me."

"You don't think he's a drug dealer, do you?"

"Hardly," Sandy said.

"Anyway, you've got to promise not to tell anyone about my story," I said. "And I mean *anyone*."

"I give you the famous Parker promise. My lips are sealed, unless of course you want them open for any reason."

I decided to ignore her comment. "Just don't tell anyone, okay?"

"Okay," she said, in a way that made me believe her. "I really did like your story today. I thought it was good." Then she paused.

"Don't stop now, tell me more—oops—" I said, accidentally bumping up against her as I stumbled on a hole in the field.

She pushed back against me. "You'd better watch it, or I'll tell you something you don't know."

"Like what?"

"Change the subject, Sandra," she told herself in an officious voice. "Did you decide where you're going to college yet?"

I laughed. "No, did you?"

"Not really," she said. "I figure my grades are good enough to get into Stanford, if I'm lucky. I can major in political science and join the diplomatic corps. I'd really like to work in another country one day."

"Really? That sounds like fun."

"I think so." Then she asked. "Have you ever thought about getting married?"

It's lucky she couldn't see the expression on my face. "Why?"

"I have," she said.

"But I thought you were going to college," I said.

"I am, but later on. I think women should work if they want to, and not at home, either. After I get my degree and after I get my job somewhere in Europe, I figure I'll get married."

"To a count or something, I bet."

"Be serious," she said. "I've already got my wedding dress picked out—"

"You're kidding? You know your dress?"

"Sure, I found it in an issue of *Modern Bride* last year. My mother said she'd make it for me when the time comes. She's getting me a hope chest for Christmas, too."

"You've got to find the guy first."

"Oh, I will," she said, a little too knowingly, as we walked from the darkness across the lighted 7-Eleven parking lot.

"What're you going to get?" I asked her, checking the cars in the lot for any that I knew.

"Well, since you've picked a place renowned for its cuisine," she joked, "let's pig out tonight. Why don't we get a couple of burritos, a bag of nacho-flavored Doritos and a carton of jalapeño dip, and a box of Ding Dongs for dessert? What do you want to drink? A chocolate shake?"

My mouth was hanging open by then. "Um, well, I—uh—"

"It's okay, Allan. I'm just teasing," she said, as I opened the glass door. "Actually, I'm getting a diet Coke to drink with the saltines I have in my purse. But you can have anything you want. It's on me."

By the time we walked back to the school and went our separate ways, I realized something that I had suspected for a while: being with Sandy was fun. If she looked like Sue, I would have asked her out in a flash. But everyone knew, you just didn't date fat girls.

Chapter Fifteen

I tried to call C.J. a few more times on Saturday, using the number Sandy had given me. Every time, I heard the same recording. I couldn't imagine what was wrong, but I have to admit that I didn't have time to worry. I was more concerned about my Party House and what would happen if it fell through.

Big Story Evaporates
TEEN REPORTER TAKES LIFE

I kept asking myself whose life I was going to take, mine or C.J.'s? I should've known I couldn't count on him.

I spent the day brainstorming new blockbuster ideas. By the time I was through, I had five pages of fascinating doodles and two marginal story ideas. I could write an exposé of the graffiti in the school johns, which the Comp would never approve, or a three-part series on the effect of soap operas on high school students, which I'd never be able to write for lack of interest. I realized that I was going to have to face Miss Compton on

Monday, tell her my blockbuster had fallen through and plead for her mercy and some big story ideas.

Once I realized that I had no other options, I felt relieved in a way—the way a condemned man feels when his last chance for a reprieve has been denied. I ate dinner with my family, then settled down for a heavy HBO involvement. I was halfway through a Clint Eastwood movie when the phone rang. I glanced at my watch. Seven-thirty.

"It's for you," my mother announced.

"Hello?" I asked, half expecting to hear Sandy's voice. Instead, it was C.J.

"Hi, what's going on?" he said, as if nothing was unusual.

"Where have you been?" I asked. "Are you okay?"

"I'm fine," he said. "Something came up, that's all. Anyway, what about tonight? We're still going, aren't we?"

I was stunned by his casual tone. "Well, uh, I don't know. I guess." Suddenly the headline for my Party House story flashed back into my mind. I could write it after all. "I'm ready anytime you get here."

"What makes you think I'm going to drive?" he asked, sounding annoyed. "Just because I have a car?"

Now I was angry. "C.J., that's what you told me at school on Monday. You said you'd drive."

"I know what I said, and I never said that," he explained. "Anyway, I can't drive because the car's in the shop. What about you?"

"I don't know if—" I saw my resurrected story—and my fame—fading. "Well, maybe I can get one of our cars," I offered. "I'll just say I need it for a story. Hang on."

My mother and the Duke hardly batted an eye. They were too busy getting ready for some party to ask many questions.

"Where are you going?" the Duke asked.

"This kid's house, off Camelback Road. Not too far. I need to interview him and some friends about their experiences at ASU." I figured there had to be some Arizona State students there. "I won't be out late."

The Duke thought a moment and nodded. "Be back by eleven," he said.

"Fine." I quickly agreed, because I knew the curfew didn't matter. They wouldn't be home by eleven.

When I got back to the phone, C.J. said, "Let's just forget tonight." Now he sounded awful.

"Don't hang up," I almost yelled. "Are you all right?" I asked. More silence. "C.J.?"

Finally, he spoke.

"What?" he asked quietly.

"Look, I'm coming by to pick you up. What's your address?"

He was silent.

"Where are you?"

"I'll be at the Seventh Avenue Diner." He was almost mumbling.

"At Indian School Road?"

"Yeah."

"Will you be inside?" I asked.

"Where do you think I'll be?" he snapped.

"No, I mean—" I said, then thought better of it. I had too many questions to ask, too much to say to begin now. "I'll be there in ten minutes," I added.

I was there in eight.

I had no sooner parked in the diner's lot, when someone tapped on the front passenger's window. I jumped a mile.

Then C.J.'s face loomed into view.

I leaned over and pushed the door open. "What're you doing out here?" I asked. "I thought you were going to be inside."

"I saw you drive up," he said, getting in.

"Where have you been this week?" I asked. "I've been worried about you. I tried to call you all week."

His eyebrows raised. "How? You don't know my number," he said.

"Oh, yes, I do. I talked to your father—I'm sure it was your father—and he said you don't live at home anymore."

"So? What if I don't?" he asked. "Actually, it's none of your business."

"C.J.—"

"Okay, so I don't live at home. I thought everyone at school knew that."

"I didn't know that," I told him. "Until I found out that you live with your aunt."

He looked at me, definitely surprised.

"I thought you knew," he said quickly.

"I don't believe you," I said.

"No, really, I thought I told you."

"I still don't believe you."

"Then don't believe me," he replied. I hoped he might say something else then, but in typical C.J. fashion, he changed the subject. "Hey, it's too early for the Party House. Why don't we get something to eat first? Want to go in?"

I wasn't in the mood for anything but the truth, but I didn't feel like arguing anymore. We walked inside the Seventh Avenue Diner, a plastic all-night restaurant covered inside and out in bright yellow.

Business was slow, and service was fast. As soon as we sat down, a waitress wanted our order.

"I'll take a small Coke," I told her.

"There's a two-dollar minimum per person at night," she replied.

"Okay, give me a large order of fries and a large Coke," I said.

"Cheeseburger platter with onion rings and a chocolate shake," C.J. ordered. "This place is a real rip-off," he continued as soon as the waitress was gone. "I can't believe they have a minimum. It's hardly the Ritz." I watched him talk. He was playing with the cream pitcher, flipping its top open, then closing it. "I think this is sour. Can you believe it? They're trying to kill us."

He looked at me then, and I shrugged. "I don't care if they do," I said. "I just want to know what's going on. You haven't been in school since Monday."

"I told you something came up," he said calmly. "What else is there to say?"

"The whole story, for starters," I said.

"You can stop playing Mr. Reporter with me and stop asking questions. This is my life we're talking about, not one of your stories."

"Can't I ask a friend a question?"

"Not if the friend says to butt out," he told me.

I sighed and shut up. We stared at each other, waiting for our food.

After a few seconds he volunteered some information. "I left home in May." Then he added, "It's no big deal."

"Maybe not to you, but it is to me," I said.

He shrugged and fiddled with the creamer again.

I continued, "I know there's more to it than that, because I got your aunt's phone number and I know it's disconnected. Then you call me tonight and act like everything's fine and you want to go out. Why weren't you in school? Would you tell me what's going on? And why's her phone disconnected? If you tell me that, I won't ask any more questions."

He flipped the creamer top again and avoided looking at me. "It's all so boring and trite. My mother died when I was four, my father got remarried, his new wife hated me, we had a lot of bad times. They got divorced when I was twelve, then last January my father got married to this woman—are you counting? This is his third wife—she's young enough to be my sister. Then she gets pregnant, and she doesn't want me around. Does this sound like a soap opera or what?" he asked. He had recited his story as if he were a remedial student who had been forced to memorize some boring soliloquy from Shakespeare. "This woman tried everything to get me out of the house. She had this way of clearing her throat that told you everything you needed to know. Like, 'Drop dead, jerk.' She went through my room, trying to find stuff. She hates me. And my father didn't care. So last May we had a fight, and I told him he was a jerk. I kind of blew up. Then I decided to move out."

"He let you move out?"

He paused a moment, as if he wasn't sure what to say. "They couldn't stand me there," he said. "So I moved in with my aunt."

"So you went to New York with her? I always thought that you went with your parents."

"What is this?" he asked. "The Spanish Inquisition?"

"No, I'm working for the *National Enquirer* these days," I joked.

"No comment," he said, as if he were running for office.

At first, I thought he was joking. But as the silence grew, I realized he was serious. Finally, our food arrived, and we ate in silence.

"Did I tell you my aunt got me an Apple computer?" he said a while later, as he bit into an onion ring.

I shook my head, disappointed that he couldn't be honest. "Is that why you weren't in school this week?"

"It's really great," he said, as if he hadn't heard me. "Maybe you can see it one of these days. You want these?" he asked, pointing to a few soggy french fries on my plate. I noticed he had finished his onion rings and had drained his shake.

"They're not very good," I said, but he took them anyway. After he had finished them, I watched him lick his finger and pick up tiny pieces of onion ring from his plate. Then he sucked them into his mouth.

"Is everything all right?" I asked him.

"Everything's fine," he said, picking up more onion-ring crumbs. "Don't I sound like I'm having a good time?" He didn't wait for an answer. "I can't stand it," he said suddenly. "I just can't stand it. Let's get out of here. I've got to talk to someone or I'll get even crazier."

"All right," I said, getting out of our booth. "Let me figure out the bill." I looked at the check the waitress had left. "Let's see—"

"Allan, you've got to pay for me," C.J. told me then.

"What?" I wasn't sure if I understood what he meant.

"I'm broke," he told me.

Then he turned and walked outside.

Chapter Sixteen

By the time I caught up with him, C.J. was standing by my car.

"Why didn't you tell me you were broke before you ordered? What if I didn't have enough money?" I told him. "I would've loaned you some money if you needed it—I just like advance warning."

"You trust me?" he joked. "For the money?"

"Yes," I admitted, getting in the car and unlocking C.J.'s door. "I trust you."

"You're sure? I mean, I already owe you ten bucks. Because if you don't, we could always go to downtown Phoenix and sell my blood," he said.

"What?"

"I'll go sell my blood," he repeated.

"You wouldn't do that, would you?"

"Why not?" he asked. "Only you can't do it very often."

"Are you joking?" I asked, afraid that I was finally hearing the truth.

He shrugged. "Maybe. Who knows? Maybe one day you'll find out."

I rolled down my window to get some fresh air.

"I thought I was going to find out now. That's what you said inside."

We sat silently for a while.

"I told you I don't live at home," he said finally. "You talked to my father. You heard what he sounded like." He sighed and continued, "It gets complicated. When I left home last May, my father called the cops and said I ran away. That's against the law, so they arrested me and they put me on probation. But I didn't want to live at home, so my father said I could live with my aunt. My aunt's not like I said. She doesn't have any money, we didn't travel anywhere. I lied about all that, because I can't stand it. She has five kids, no money, a crummy house. She lets me stay there. I sleep on a mattress in her garage."

"But there's no heat in a garage," I said, thinking about our occasional forty-degree nights.

He nodded his head. "You're right. I freeze a lot at night."

"What about gas for your car? How do you get money for that?"

"It's not my car," he said. "It's *her* car." Then he looked away and said quietly, "And I only used it once, that first day of school."

I was stunned. "How could you act like it was yours? You let me say all kinds of things about that car, and you never told me?"

"It sounded better," he said. "I wanted a car. I wanted everyone to think I had a car. But you believed me so much that you wanted rides, so I had to make up excuses."

"No wonder you didn't want me to write a story about you. How could you do that to me? I thought we were friends."

"We are. I just wish I hadn't gotten into this mess. I wish my mother hadn't died. I wish my father loved me. I wish I had money. I wish I could buy things like you do. I wish I had a family like yours. I wish, I wish, I wish. But none of it does any good. I'm no one, I'm nothing. I'm going nowhere."

"But what about college?"

He rubbed his fingers together. "Money," he said. "Moola. Dinero. How am I going to pay for it?" Then he laughed. "You probably think I drink a lot or that I like parties, that that's the reason I know about the Party House."

"Well, I wondered...."

"I heard some kids talking about it at school, and I heard where it was. The reason I started going there was—" He laughed again; he sounded embarrassed. "It was for the food. The food! Can you believe it?" He was indignant.

I tried to lighten his mood. "Yeah, I noticed that you like to eat."

"With my aunt's kids there's never enough. You thought I went to Taco Bell on Monday. I don't eat lunch at school anymore. I don't have the money. She used to give me some, but she lost her job last month. There's no money for lunches, for anything. So I said I was going on errands just so you wouldn't know. Do you know what it's like not to eat from breakfast to dinner? Or to live on peanut-butter sandwiches and pancakes? Sometimes my stomach growls so much I think I'm part lion."

"But you haven't told me what happened this week? Why'd you miss school?"

He looked at his watch. "Because I decided I couldn't handle school anymore."

"But you'll be there Monday, won't you?"

He looked at me then, and I thought he was going to cry.

"I'm leaving town."

"What? But—but—" I sputtered.

"There's no money, and I can't live with my aunt. It's not fair to her and her kids. And I can't move home. So I can either go to a juvenile home or I can disappear until I'm eighteen. That's when my records are sealed. So I'm leaving town."

"But isn't—"

He cut me off. "There's nothing to talk about. Anyway, if you still want to go to the Party House, we should get going."

"You could come and live with us," I volunteered.

"You're parents don't have custody of me; my aunt does. They're not family. I would have to go to a juvenile home while everything was being settled. That could take months. Anyway, your parents don't want me."

"But you're not going to leave now, are you?"

He laughed. "Are you worried about your story?"

"No!" I practically yelled. "I'm worried about you. Where would you go?"

"I'm a big boy," he said. "I can take care of myself."

"Why don't you wait a couple of days?" I asked, hoping that I could think of something to change his mind.

He shrugged. "Maybe." Then he said, "If you don't get out of this parking lot, you'll never get your story."

"This is a better story," I told him.

"After I disappear, it's all yours," was all he said.

Within ten minutes, we were at the Party House. As it turned out, the Party House was near Camelback Mountain, but despite the rich neighborhood, we had to drive down a dirt road lined with orange groves to get there.

"Maybe I should wait in the car for a while," I told him as we approached a long line of parked cars. The house was isolated, maybe on three or four acres of land.

"If you're going to write a story," C.J. said, "you should look around as much as you can. You could walk around the house and check it out."

I parked in back of the last car. Then, while C.J. headed for the front door, I walked to the side of the house, glancing in windows as I passed. I could hear the bass guitar of the old Rolling Stones tracks that were playing on the tape deck.

I opened the side gate and walked into the backyard. A few kids were there, sitting by the shallow end of the drained pool. I stepped onto the patio, trying to get a better look at the party inside, when a guy stepped to the door and stared at me, face-to-face.

"Bored with it, too?" he asked, sliding the door open. He was a cowboy in glasses, and he carried the remnants of a six-pack in one hand and an open can of beer in the other.

I backed up and tried to act calm. "No, not really," I said.

"Not really," he said, mimicking my voice. He motioned me toward the pool. There, he sat on the edge, hanging his feet into the empty pool. I chose the diving board to perch on. The more I looked at him, the more I could tell he was older, and drunker, than I had thought. "This bunch really gets on my nerves."

"Yeah?" I said.

"Yeah?" he snapped again. "They party every weekend," he said, pointing at the house. "But at least they're going to get out of school. I'm still trying."

I looked at him, but I wasn't asking any questions this time.

"I'm almost twenty years old," he complained, "and I'm still trying to graduate."

"You haven't graduated?" I asked, unable to stop myself.

"Nope. They held me back two years in first grade," he said, shaking two fingers at me. "Two years! And I've been doing a good job of messing things up on my own ever since."

"Where do you go?"

"Ocotillo," he said.

"You're kidding. That's where I go."

"I know. But I bet you don't know me."

I shook my head.

"Herb Coombs," he said, and reached toward the diving board. We shook hands. He crushed mine in his grip.

"Your name sounds familiar, but I never saw you—I don't think."

"You were in World Geography with me a couple of years ago," he said.

"I was?"

"Yep, but I guess I didn't exactly have perfect attendance," he said, then finished his can of beer and threw it into the swimming pool. It clattered toward the drain. "Antottle, right? I've seen your stuff in the school paper." I nodded. "Got a match?"

"I don't smoke," I told him.

"Thought so." He patted his pockets. "Well, what do you know?" He pulled a book of matches from his rear pocket. Then he took a cigarette from his shirt pocket and lit it.

"What're you doing here?" he asked, as he exhaled.

"Well, I was invited."

"Invited? That's a good one." He pulled the top on another beer. "What I want to do is join the Air Force, but they won't take me till I graduate. Here," he said, offering me a beer again.

"I don't want any," I told him.

"Why'd you come to this party anyway?"

Even if I didn't drink any, I knew I had to take a beer. I shrugged. "Okay," I said. "Thanks." I took the can he offered and popped it open, fully expecting to see the police drive up at any minute. I had to find C.J. and get inside.

"See you," I said, but Herb didn't hear. Then I walked to the sliding door and peered in. The room was crowded with what looked like a thousand kids. It was filled with smoke and noise and beer. I couldn't see C.J., but I went inside anyway. I sidestepped my way through the crowd and headed for the far side of the room, when I suddenly saw C.J. standing near the entrance to the kitchen talking to someone.

As I started to walk toward him, I impulsively glanced at the couch. It was one of those moments that happen just by chance. Seated there, beer bottle in hand, Brian Sawyer was in a passionate clinch with some girl. It took me only a moment longer to realize that he was kissing Vicky Lincoln.

By then I had reached C.J.

"Do you know who that is?" I asked C.J., motioning in Brian's direction.

"Who?" C.J. asked.

"The Casanova on the couch."

"Oh, yeah," he said. "This is his house."

The headline on my story suddenly loomed much larger:

TEEN BULLY RUNS PARTY HOUSE
Surprise Girlfriend Writes
High School Gossip Column

I had to get out of there before they saw me.

Chapter Seventeen

No sooner had I thought of leaving, than Vicky opened her eyes and looked right at me. As I turned to leave, I said, "Come on, let's get out of here." The last people I wanted to see up close and personal were Vicky and Brian.

"What's wrong?" C.J. asked, as I practically pushed him ahead of me out the front door.

"That's Brian Sawyer," I told him. "Don't you know who he is?"

"The guy who owns the house?"

"And he's with Vicky Lincoln."

"Just a second," he said. By then we were outside, but C.J. opened the door and walked back in. I headed for the car.

A moment later, C.J. returned, holding up his prize, an unopened bottle of champagne and two Dixie cups.

"What are you going to do with that?" I asked, as he got in the car.

"Shampoo my dog," he said and grinned.

"You don't have a dog," I said. "And what if a cop stops us? We could be arrested."

"You're right," he said. "And I know what'll happen to me if he does. But I'm willing to take that chance."

"Well, at least put it under the seat," I said. "And don't even think about opening it in the car."

"All right, all right."

I started the engine and drove back onto the dirt road that led to Camelback.

"I can't believe this is Brian's house," I told him.

"Right," C.J. said. "If nothing else, you can blackmail him."

That's when I realized the predicament I was in. The last person I wanted to blackmail was Brian. He had really behaved since the incident in P.E. But I had to write the story. Discovering that he ran the Party House gave me no pleasure at all. I couldn't have imagined a worse ending to the story.

In a few minutes, I was driving down Indian School Road, approaching a shopping center with a Safeway supermarket. "Why don't you pull in here?" C.J. asked. Then he explained, "So we can talk." As I drove into the lot, he directed, "Go around to the side. Nobody's over there."

With that, he pulled the bottle of champagne from under his seat.

"C.J.—really—"

But he popped the cork anyway. Mist swirled from the bottle neck.

"Please throw it out," I told him.

Instead, he poured champagne into the two Dixie cups. Then, after I had parked the car in a deserted area near the Safeway dumpster, he handed me a Dixie cup of champagne.

"I don't want this," I told him, refusing to take it. "What if a cop comes?"

"Just hold it. Can't you pretend? You can throw it out the window if the cops show up."

"Okay," I said, taking the cup.

"To friends," he said, pretending to clink glasses. He sipped his champagne, while I held mine. "Now what we need is some caviar, and we'd be all set."

"You've never had caviar," I said, looking at the bubbles fizzing in my champagne.

He was silent a moment as he took another drink. Then he looked at me. "You're right," he said. "I've never had caviar. But I will." He drank some more. "One day, I'm going to have caviar. And I'll go to New York and L.A. and Santa Fe. I'll be able to go anywhere I want."

He filled his Dixie cup again.

"You're no fun," he said. "This could be the last time you see me—I could decide to leave tonight—and you won't even drink to my success."

I took a sip. The taste of sour, bubbly grape juice filled my mouth. "Okay, are you happy?"

"That wasn't so bad, was it?"

I shrugged and took another sip. "I don't want you to run away."

"There's nothing you can do," C.J. said. "I shouldn't even have told you."

"I thought we were friends." I drank some more.

"Do you know what it's like to have a father who hates you? Not to have a home? I've been trying to work everything out, but it's hard when you're sixteen."

"But can't you just explain everything to the police?"

"Look, he reported me as a runaway minor. You can go to Fort Grant for that. That's already on my record. So if my aunt can't take care of me, the state will. And I couldn't handle that. No way. No way at all."

As I finished my cup of champagne, he added, "You have to promise me something."

"What?"

"That you won't tell anyone anything about what's going on with me. I mean nobody. Anyone could turn me in. For all I know, you could."

"Why would I do that?" I asked. "We're friends."

He filled his cup with champagne and then filled mine. "I wish we could stay like this forever."

"What do you mean?" I asked, then chuckled. "In the Safeway parking lot, next to the dumpster?"

"No, like this," he said. "Talking, having a good time."

"Then why do I feel like it's the night before an execution?"

Suddenly he opened the door and got out of the car, holding the champagne bottle. The next thing I knew, he had thrown the bottle toward the dumpster. The bottle sailed inside and smashed on the bottom.

C.J. poked his head through the open car window and said, "I'll try to call you tomorrow." Then he walked around the rear of the car. I don't know why, but I thought he was coming around to my side. I waited a moment, then turned around to look for him. But I didn't see him anywhere.

I started to panic. Too much was happening, and I wasn't sure what to do. I noticed an alley behind my car that emptied into the parking lot. I wedged the cup between my legs and quickly started the car. I accelerated and spun the wheel until my car was facing the alley. All I saw were tumbleweeds, bleached by my headlights, staring back.

I drove down the alley until I reached the next street. Then I drove around the shopping center once more. But C.J. had disappeared.

I was angry with myself for allowing him to leave. Then I did something I came to regret: out of anger or frustration, I picked up my second cup of champagne and finished it. I didn't even want it, but I drank it anyway. Then I drove home.

Fortunately, my parents were still at a party down the street when I got there. I was feeling no pain from the champagne, as I maneuvered myself out of the Buick and up the driveway past our Ford. I felt dizzy for a second and stopped to lean on the car. The hood was hot. Rich, I was sure, had been up to his tricks again.

"I know what you've been doing," I told him when I walked into the family room. He was sprawled in the recliner watching *Chiller Theater*.

"Yeah, watching TV."

"I know you took the car again," I said, sitting at the bar as a dizzy spell overcame me.

"You didn't see me."

"The h-hood on the car is hot," I said, my head spinning. "Mom and Dad'll believe me."

"You tell them that, and I'll tell them you came home drunk."

I inhaled quickly. "I did not," I said.

"Then how come you have booze breath? I can smell you all the way over here."

"I never go drinking. I don't do things like that. They won't believe you. You're the one who's always stealing the car. Or going off to the bedroom with Patti when they're not home."

"Where's *your* girlfriend?" Rich snapped. "You can't even get a date. Sue Arnold couldn't take you more than once. So you took out that pig last night."

I thought I was flying across the room at him, trying to wring his neck. But I ended up on the floor looking up at him.

"Why don't you go to bed and forget the whole thing?" he said.

"But what if you got in an accident?" I asked, trying to lift myself up.

"What if you got picked up for drinking?" he countered.

I was trapped by my own brother. "Okay, you win. But I'm not getting drunk anymore, so you better not take the car again."

"You'll never know it, if I do," he said.

"Oh, Rich, why can't you—"

But before I could finish, I felt myself getting sick, and I ran to the bathroom just in time.

Chapter Eighteen

Sunday, I kept waiting for C.J. to call. The few times the phone rang, I practically jumped out of my skin. But he never called, and I didn't know if I would ever see him again.

To take my mind off everything, I tried to write my Party House story. Nothing seemed quite right, but I kept plugging away. I told myself that if I kept working on it all day, I'd reward myself later. After dinner, I had three good pages and four mediocre ones. So I decided to keep my promise: I would go to Cactus Drugs to see if the new *Playboy* had arrived.

"If C.J. calls, tell him I'll call him back," I told my mother. "Get his number. Or tell him to call me back in an hour. I'm going to Cactus Drugs."

I didn't even bother asking for the car. I just headed for the garage and Rich's bike. In ten minutes I was at the drugstore.

If I hadn't known better, I would've thought Sandy had been waiting for me. No sooner had I parked myself at the magazine rack, seen that the new issue of *Playboy* hadn't arrived, and begun to peruse *Fangoria* when she turned the feminine hygiene corner, heading toward the deodorant aisle.

"Allan, what're you doing here?" she said, approaching me.

"Using the library," I said.

My eyes darted to the two boxes of feminine protection she was holding. "One of the joys of life," she said, indicating the boxes. "They're having a sale." I think she could tell that I wasn't ready for this kind of conversation, so she changed the topic. "What're you reading?"

I showed her the cover, with its photograph of a bloody head and bursting eyeball from some current horror movie. "It's very educational," I quipped.

"How can you read that?"

"Who reads? I just look at the pictures," I joked.

"I thought that's what you boys do with *Playboy*," she teased back.

"There's a lot to read in that," I said.

"If you read Braille," she said, then smiled. "Why don't we get something to eat?"

My first response was to say no. "Well, I've got my brother's bike, I—"

"We can put it in the back seat of my car. Anyway, I think you need a treat today. Besides, if you won't come with me, I'll have to kidnap you."

"You believe in committing crimes?"

"What? Adultery?"

"Don't you have to be married to commit that?"

"Well?" she asked.

I laughed—uncomfortably.

"Let's go," Sandy suggested, grabbing the sleeve of my jacket and pulling me toward the checkout counter.

"I should be home by eight," I told her, checking my watch. It was almost seven-thirty.

"You know what I want?" she asked me when we had stashed Rich's bike in her car and driven down Camelback Road. "A huge hot-fudge sundae."

I looked at her skeptically. "But think of all the calories."

"I'm past worrying about those. This is the real me," she said, grabbing a bunch of her jacket, pretending that it was her fleshy side.

I took a chance and said, "Come on, you could lose it."

"Sure, sure. I looked at myself in the mirror the other day and wondered what it'd be like to have a figure like Brooke Shields. I decided that wouldn't be any fun at all. Besides, I'd probably end up with a brain like hers, too. Anyway, I kind of like myself the way I am."

We were both quiet. I wanted to tell her about C.J., but I remembered what he had told me. I kept my mouth shut. "I probably should go home soon," I reminded her.

"You're no fun sometimes, Allan. One time I really am going to kidnap you and make you have some fun."

I shifted uncomfortably in my seat. She kept driving. Then, as we started past Camelback Mountain, she made a quick left turn and headed toward the slope.

"Where're you going?" I asked her.

"I told you I was going to kidnap you sometime," she said. "You've just been kidnapped."

"Yeah, are you going to violate me, too?" I asked sarcastically.

"I'm more worried that you're the one who'll get some ideas," Sandy said.

"Then why're you taking me up here if you're worried what I'll do?" I reasoned.

"Maybe I like to get myself into difficult situations."

"Anyway, what kind of ideas would I get?" I asked, as she parked the car.

"I don't know, you might want to take advantage of the situation, or me—you know what I mean? I've never been up here alone with a guy before."

"Methinks you doth protest too much," I said.

"Briggs'd love you for that quote," she said. By now, her thigh rested against mine, and I was contemplating jumping out of the car.

"Are you ticklish?" she asked suddenly. "*I'm* not."

That sounded like an innocent enough question. I took the bait. "Oh, I bet you are," I said. "Everybody is, a little."

"Try me."

I tried to dig into her waist, but it was hard to make a dent through her down jacket.

"You're not even trying," she complained.

"Well, okay." I felt as if I had to win by tickling her. "I'll fix you this time."

I tried to attack both sides of her stomach, but she was laughing so hard that I couldn't tell if I was tickling her or not.

"My turn," she said, and laughed again. Her fingers were jabbing my side before I knew it and could stop her. I was laughing despite the pain.

"Hey... hey... stop it!" I gasped, in between laughs.

"You can't stop me!"

I put my left arm around her shoulders and grabbed her left wrist. Then with my right hand I grasped her other wrist.

"Okay," I said, through clenched teeth, "I stopped it."

But she looked at me, through the tangle of arms, she merely looked at me and said, "See? What did I tell you? I knew I couldn't trust you."

We both started laughing again, and I released her wrists. I started to take my arm from around her, but she said, "You can leave it there, if you want." Before I could decide whether to move it or not, she rested her head on my arm.

I held my breath for a moment, not quite sure what was happening. Then she swiveled her head toward me until our noses were almost touching. She leaned forward and kissed me. I wasn't exactly surprised, but I wasn't sure what to do next.

"Did I do something dumb?" she asked, starting to pull away.

I wasn't sure what to say. "You're kind of crazy, you know."

"I know," she said, and swooped for another kiss. Then she reached for the zipper on my jacket and pulled it down.

"Um, what're you doing?" I asked, squirming in my seat. I wasn't sure I was ready for any of this.

By then, she was unbuttoning my shirt.

"I have to see if Brian was right," she said. "Why're you wearing an undershirt?"

"Oh, I—"

"That was a rhetorical question, Allan," she said, tugging at my shirt. "You don't have to answer." Then her fingers were rippling through my chest hair, galvanizing every nerve. "I don't know why you'd feel self-conscious about this, Allan. You look great."

I kissed her back then.

"What time is it?" I asked, when I realized it must be late.

"Does it matter?" she said and gave me another kiss that left me faint.

"I really do have to be home," I told her, struggling to look at my watch. "I'll get in trouble with my parents."

"But I kind of like this," she said, kissing my neck.

"Don't give me a hickey," I warned her, trying to sit up straight.

"We'll have to do it again sometime," she said. "You're going to have to ask me out again."

Then I said, "Well, play your cards right and maybe I'll ask you to Homecoming."

As soon as I heard the words, I knew I'd made a mistake, but I was caught up in the passion of the moment.

"Oh, Allan, I'd love to go, I really would." She squeezed me tightly and kissed me again.

"That's nice," I said dumbly. I hadn't meant to ask her. I'd been teasing, but she had taken me seriously.

"We'll have a great time," she said. She kissed me again, then started the car.

We should have gotten the hot-fudge sundae.

Chapter Nineteen

On Monday, everyone at school was gearing up for Homecoming on Friday. Booster signs, like Douse the Suns and Burn Up the Sundowners, had been plastered everywhere, and special tables had been set up in every hallway to sell tickets to the Homecoming dance. But I walked right by two tables on the way to my locker that morning. I didn't know if I was going to Homecoming or not. Still, my lips felt puckery from my kissing session with Sandy. If I took her to Homecoming, there would be more kisses to follow.

On the way to first hour, Ginger D'Angelo even cornered me in the hall.

"Hey, Allan," she called, stopping me in my tracks, "do you want to buy a Homecoming ticket from me?" She had a handful of ten-dollar tickets.

"I don't know," I told her.

"Really? I thought you'd be taking Sue," she said. I only wished I could. "You two make a real cute couple," she added.

That was a thought: I could forget Sandy and take Sue. I was sure Sue would kiss even better. If Ginger was any indication, maybe there was hope for Sue and me, after all. "Well, I'll let you know if I want a ticket."

"Just remember," she called as I continued on my way to P.E., "if you decide to go to the dance, buy your ticket from me."

I wondered how Brian would react to me in P.E., but he wasn't there. We continued working on our swimming unit.

Ever since the first day when I had forgotten my contact lens case and had to run laps with Brian, I had made sure I didn't make that mistake again. I would dutifully take my lenses out at the beginning of the hour, put them in my case and then replace them after I had showered. Monday, though, I lost my right contact. I had taken both lenses out at the beginning of the hour as usual, but when I went to insert them after class, my right lens was missing. I would've blamed Brian, if only he had been there. Maybe I took it out too quickly and wasn't careful about putting it in the case. I wasn't sure. All I knew was that without my contacts or my glasses, which were collecting dust on my dresser at home, I would need a white cane and a seeing-eye dog to make it through the day.

Fortunately, I could spend second hour in the nurse's office, trying to reach my mother. If nothing else, she could drop off my glasses. I wasn't thrilled about the prospect of wearing them, but they were better than blindness. But she wasn't home, no matter how many times I let the phone ring. And at the end of second hour, the nurse politely told me I would have to go to class.

I groped my way to homeroom. As I sat down, I squinted at the fuzzy void of C.J.'s desk. I brought my watch within an inch of my face to read the time. He had two minutes till the final bell.

He never came.

As I walked into English next hour, a large blur lumbered toward me.

"How are you this morning?" Sandy asked, in a special way that made me cringe.

I shrugged. "Okay, I guess."

"What's wrong with your eyes?" she asked.

"I lost a contact. And I can't get ahold of my mother to bring me my glasses."

"Can you read?"

"Yeah, if the paper's about six inches from my nose."

"Good, you can practice on this," she said, handing me a note:

Good morning!

My mother and I are going shopping for a dress tonight. Actually, we'll probably just buy a pattern and the material and make it ourselves. She has been promising me a new dress for a long time, so I took advantage of the situation. Also, she said I can have a party at my house after the dance. Won't that be fantastic? I've started the guest list (sounds kind of fancy, huh?). Answer right away.
Your Abductress,
Sandy

By the time I had finished reading it, I wished I had been struck totally blind. Fortunately, I couldn't answer, with the warden lording over us. We were supposed to be listening to Richard Burton read sections of *The Scarlet Letter*, and Briggs was watching us like a hawk for signs of disinterest.

Right after class, Sandy asked me, "Isn't it great about the party? I can't believe my mother's letting me do this—it's not like her to be so generous, you know."

I smiled weakly. I didn't know what I was going to do. Looking at Sandy then, well-illuminated under the fluorescent lights, her shape even more ill-defined by my poor vision, I could picture her grotesque body buried under a huge homemade sack of cloth at the dance. I liked her well enough to kiss her in the dark, on deserted Camelback Mountain, and I tingled at the thought of her hands rubbing my chest, but I wasn't sure I could take her to the dance in front of everyone. I saw it all in headlines:

BOY FORCED TO DATE PIG
Teenage World Stunned

Or:

Hogtied by Love:
BOY PLANS 'SUEY'-CIDE

Somehow I had lost complete control on Camelback Mountain. Now I was going to pay the price, unless I took the bull by the horns, or the pig by its tail, and stopped it.

By the time lunch came, I knew I couldn't go through with my date with Sandy. I just didn't know how I would get out of it.

As I made my way toward my usual table on the patio, a vaguely familiar blur appeared at the other end of the patio, walking toward me. I was so intent on not missing my table that I wasn't paying attention and bumped into that blurry individual, who suddenly came into focus: Harry.

I squinted to make sure I was seeing correctly.

"Huh—hi," I stuttered. He just looked at me and tried to walk past me. It was one of those awkward situations when we both tried to get around each other on the same side. We'd both move: I to my right, he to his left, and we'd be stuck still. Finally, I just froze as he scooted past, never having said a word. I tried to remember his facial expression (fear? hostility? amusement?), but I hadn't seen much of anything.

I called my mother a few minutes later. She delivered my glasses to the office just in time, before Spanish started.

With my glasses on, I felt as if I was seeing the world through fresh eyes. It didn't matter that I looked like my old Frog Eyes self. Somehow, everything looked different, and better.

When I saw Sue sitting in Spanish, looking as good as ever, I asked myself, why couldn't Sandy be as thin as Sue? And, why couldn't Sue have gone to Camelback Mountain with me, alone? Why had Harry ruined everything?

"Everybody's really worked up over Homecoming," she said, before class started. It's as if she had read my mind.

"Yeah, it's a big deal around here," I told her.

"I don't really know much about it. I went to a little high school in Chandler. We didn't have a football team or Homecoming or anything like that."

Then I opened my mouth and asked, "Do you want to go with me? It's lots of fun."

"Oh, well, let me see." I tried to detect any signs of uncertainty in her voice. "Can I tell you tomorrow?"

"Yeah, or you could call me tonight. Or I could call you."

"I'm going to be busy tonight," she said. "I'll tell you tomorrow. If that's okay."

"Sure," I said.

"Thanks for asking," she said. Then—I could swear to it—I saw her wink at me.

Goodbye, Sandy. Hello, Sue. I was definitely going to cancel my date.

Even the *Observer* developed a good case of Homecoming fever that afternoon.

"We're building a float for Homecoming," Miss Compton announced to us in journalism. "Vicky thought it would be a good idea, and Mr. Rucker approved it this morning."

"Didn't I tell you Mr. Rucker would like it?" Vicky said, addressing everyone. Mr. Rucker was the principal. "We'll show all those other floats up."

"Now Vicky's going to handle everything," Miss Compton concluded, "so check with her some time this hour to see what work crew you're on."

I wasn't about to seek Vicky out, so I laid low. A little later she walked over to my desk.

"I put you down for the flower committee," she said quietly.

"Flowers? You're kidding?"

"I always thought you had a florid style," she tried to joke. "Depending on what you're writing."

"I don't want to do flowers," I said. I wasn't going to threaten her with my story information, but I have to admit I was thinking about it.

"I'm going to help you," she said. "Anyway, frogs like flowers. You know, lily pads and all that. You'll feel right at home."

"I'd watch what I say if I were you."

"That's a joke, Allan. All we have to do is make two thousand flowers. That's about twelve boxes of Kleenex."

"I'd rather use them to blow my nose," I told her.

"Can you stay today? So we can get started after school?"

I sensed she was up to something, and I was curious to know what it was.

"Well—" I didn't want to seem too anxious.

She patted me on the back. "Come on, be a sport."

"Sure, why not?" I agreed.

It didn't take long to find out what Vicky wanted. She had no sooner brought in a few boxes of Kleenex and an empty cardboard box for finished flowers than she looked at me and asked sweetly, "Did you have a good time Saturday night?"

"That's a question I should be asking you," I said.

She smiled tentatively. "Touché."

"Anyway, you'll see what I thought when I finish writing my story on the Party House."

That got her. "Why do you want to write a story about it?" she demanded.

"Why did you want to write about me being Frog Eyes for your column?"

"I write a gossip column," she explained.

"Well, I write the truth. And if Brian Sawyer is running the Party House, then I'm going to write about it."

"Who had a beer in his hand?" she snapped.

"I wasn't drinking it," I told her. "Anyway, for all you know, I might have been throwing away someone else's empty can."

"So you're just going to put our names in the paper? Compton won't let you."

"Whatever I do, you'll get to read it when it's printed," I said. Actually, I hadn't planned on using names at all.

"*If* it gets printed. You don't even know the truth about everything."

"Like what don't I know? That you and Brian are seeing each other? That'd be a good item for your column."

She grimaced. "If you write that it's Brian's house, you're wrong. It's not his place."

"Then whose house is it?"

She stopped and thought a moment. "I guess it doesn't matter," she said. "Brian's parents are divorced; his father moved to Alaska. The house belongs to the boyfriend of Brian's mother. It's *his* house. He lets Brian use it when he wants to spend the night with Mrs. Sawyer."

Now that was lousy. "Are you sure?"

"What do you think?" she asked sarcastically. "So why don't you print that, too? He pays Brian money to get lost and gives him the keys to his house. How do you think that makes Brian feel?"

"I'm not using any names, but I have to write the story," I said.

That wasn't what she wanted to hear. "Why do you hate Brian so much?" she asked then.

"Me? He gives me the hard time. Do you think I wanted to find him at the Party House? Hardly. That's his big mistake, not mine. But I'm not out to get him. I'm just writing about a house where there happens to be parties. And—like I said—I'm not mentioning names."

Vicky stood up. "Okay, if that's the way you want it," she said. "I've got to go see him. I'll be back later."

As I began to work, Louie Howard pushed a janitor's cart into the library. Louie attended special-education classes at school and worked as a janitorial assistant afterward. He was the one pictured in last year's yearbook assembling a model car as part of a unit on automotive skills. Besides being retarded, which was enough of a handicap, Louie was also known for his feet: he had twelve toes, six on each foot.

About every other day, somebody at lunch would coax Louie to take off his shoes and socks and display his toes. I had seen Brian encourage him a couple of times. As Louie removed his shoes and socks, thinking that the world would magically open up to him and that the boys would no longer steal his books or put his underwear in the foot powder box in P.E., someone would yell, "Look, Louie's going to show his toes. God, how gross! Just look at them."

Then someone else would throw Louie's shoes and socks across the cafeteria. Girls would shriek if one landed near them, as if they were contaminated with contagious six-toed microbes. Long after everyone else had left the cafeteria, Louie would still be barefoot hunting his shoes and socks. But a day or so later, when they asked for a repeat performance, Louie would willingly oblige.

As he swept around my table that afternoon, I found myself staring at his shoes. Were they larger than mine? Did he have trouble wearing socks? How did he wear sandals?

"Hi," he said. "Those pretty," he added, pointing to the tissue carnations.

"Yeah," I answered.

"What are they for?"

"Homecoming." Then I explained, "It's for the football game Friday."

"And a dance, too," he said. He obviously knew more about Homecoming than I thought. "Do you play football?"

"No." I tossed another flower into the box.

"Are you going to the game?"

"I go to all of the games," I told him.

"Me, too," he said. "I like football. It's fun."

I nodded in agreement and made another flower.

"Are you going to the dance?"

"Maybe, I don't know." I felt foolish for expressing my doubts to Louie. I had decided to wait until tomorrow to explain everything to Sandy. "Are you going?"

"Oh, yes," he said. Then he asked, "Are you going with Jane?"

"Jane? Oh, *Jane*!" Jane McDonald was the head cheerleader and easily the cutest girl in school. Louie was always following her around, like a wrecked car in tow. "No, somebody else." Probably, I thought.

He watched me finish a flower.

"Do you play football?" he asked again.

"No, I don't play football."

"What are these for?" he asked, caressing one of the flowers.

"For a float. The newspaper's having a float at the game."

The conversation continued much the same way, until a janitor stopped in and told him to finish his work. Then Louie picked up his broom and swept his way across the library. A little later, I reached the end of the first box and stopped production. Vicky would have to finish them herself.

I had worked enough for one day.

Chapter Twenty

Tuesday morning, contacts in place, I headed for the j-room before school to talk to the Comp. I had finished my Party House story, and I wanted to give her plenty of time before it would appear in next Friday's paper.

"I've finished my blockbuster," I said proudly, holding a five-page story. "I thought you'd want to see it before I sent it to the printer."

"You're right," she said. "So what'd you write on?"

Just as she reached for the story, Vicky burst into the room.

"I've got the copy for my column," she announced, hurrying to Miss Compton's desk.

"You're getting later every week," the Comp said.

"There's still time to get it to the printer," Vicky said. "There're only a few changes."

"Yes, I'll run it down during my free hour this morning. But how about Monday, next week?"

"I'll try," Vicky said.

"Let me take a look at your changes," the Comp said to Vicky. "Allan, I can read your story by this afternoon, and we can talk about it during class."

"Fine," I said and aimed myself for the door.

As I walked out of the j-room, Brian was standing near the door. I guessed that he must be waiting for Vicky, but he looked as if he had lost his best friend. He wouldn't even look at me.

I was halfway down the hall when I heard Vicky's voice again. She was talking louder than usual, and I turned to look. She was standing in the hallway outside the j-room, shaking her right hand at Brian.

"—away," I heard her say. His face looked all drawn into a knot. "Stay away. I told—"

Then her voice drifted off. I wondered what was going on between the two of them. Whatever it was must have been bad, because Brian never showed up for P.E.

I had my work cut out for me in English. I had written and rewritten a note to Sandy explaining my mistake, but it never came out the way I wanted. I decided there wasn't going to be an easy way at all. So I slipped her this note midway through the hour:

Dear Sandy,

   I really don't know how to say this. No matter what I say, you'll get the wrong impression, but to be very blunt, I don't want to take you to the dance. This is awful and I feel awful, but you misunderstood me Sunday night. I wasn't really asking you; I was being sarcastic. It was just a joke. I thought you knew everything was a joke for me; you can never take me seriously. I'm sorry this ever happened. I know this isn't what you want to hear, and I know it won't be easy to take. But in five years, we'll probably both be able to laugh about it.

                                                        Allan

I think my hand was shaking a little as I gave her the note. By that time Briggs had passed out a study guide to complete. I made an effort to begin mine, but I was really only waiting to see what Sandy would do. I was sure I heard her sniff once. Then I thought she buried her head on her desk. The next thing I knew she had collected her books, placed a note very carefully on the corner of my desk and with her head drooping, went to Briggs.

"May I go to the nurse?" she whispered, without raising her head.

"What's the matter?" Briggs asked.

"I don't feel well."

"Yes, go ahead."

She quickly left the room.

I had never even considered that she might reply to my note. So I didn't want to read her note, but I couldn't stop myself:

There's nothing left to say is there? You've made up your mind and I can't change it but I don't think I'll be laughing about this in five years see you around

I wanted not to care, not to mind that she was upset. Upset? Destroyed was more like it. But I felt bad, so bad I wanted to hide.

Muppet Show Canceled:
KERMIT DUMPS MISS PIGGY!
Ex-Lovers Seek Seclusion

By lunch, word had spread among Sandy's friends that I had dumped her. I was sitting on the patio, minding my own business, when Sherry Monohan, one of Sandy's close friends, accosted me. "She made a fool of herself for you," she reproached me. "You should've never asked her out. You broke her heart."

She would have gone on, but I got up from my table and left. Already I could see what was happening:

Frog Legs for Dinner:
PIG'S FRIENDS SEEK REVENGE

I knew everything Sherry said was true, but I didn't want to hear it. My one salvation was Sue.

"What's the matter with you today?"

C.J. suddenly appeared on the other side of the table. A large knapsack was beside him.

"What are you doing here? I thought you left."

"Today," he said, as he lowered his voice. "I'm leaving today. I just wanted to say goodbye."

He looked even worse than I felt. His T-shirt was a mass of wrinkles, and even though he didn't need to shave much, he hadn't shaved in days.

"What have you been doing?"

"Sleeping in irrigation ditches," he said. "Not exactly comfortable. That's why I'm going to L.A. It's easier to get lost there. And now I have a little money."

"How'd you get that?"

"I know where my stepmother keeps some in the house. I just helped myself."

"But they'll know it was you."

"Who cares? I'm out of their life, now. Anyway, I'll be in L.A."

"What're you going to do there?" I asked.

"Hang out," he said. "Don't worry. I'll manage."

"Can't you go to a shelter or something? You don't have to sleep in ditches there, do you?"

"How do I know? I've never been there. All I know is that if I don't want to get mugged or turned over to the cops, I should stay away from the shelters. I'm not old enough for a shelter, anyway. They'd know I'm a runaway."

"Do you know anyone in L.A.?" I asked.

"My mom had a cousin there," he said, "but I don't know if he's still there. I can look him up in the phone book if I get desperate."

"But what're you going to do when your money runs out?" I asked.

He held out his hand toward me, palm up.

"What's that for?" I asked.

"You asked me what I was going to do about money." He extended his hand further. "I'll panhandle to get it."

"You will?" I asked.

"What's wrong with that?"

"Oh, C.J. . . . ." I didn't know what to say.

"Don't worry, Allan. It'll be a great adventure. But what's wrong with you?"

Somehow my problems seemed insignificant compared to his, but I briefly told him what had happened with Sandy.

"I don't know what to do," I said.

"There's nothing to do now," he said. "You've already done it."

"I know, but I feel so terrible. I really do like Sandy. It's just that—I don't know. Do you have a suggestion?"

He was looking at his watch, then. "I've got to get out of here," he said. "I'm taking the three o'clock bus, and I've got to get downtown."

"But—"

He stood up and slid his knapsack on. "You know what to do, Allan. You know how to make things right."

"I don't know."

He held out his hand, and we shook. Then he smiled. "See you when I'm eighteen."

I felt like I could cry. "Well, write me or something."

"Yeah. Sure," he said.

Then I watched him as he walked away. He turned the corner by the Science Building and vanished.

I was so depressed by C.J. and Sandy that I couldn't sit on the patio any longer. I threw my lunch out and headed for journalism to see if the Comp had read my story.

"Your story was great!" I had never heard her so ecstatic. "I have to change a few things here and there—"

Normally I would have argued, but I was too demoralized by everything to care. "The story's first-rate. I just want to ask you one question."

"What?"

"It's true, isn't it? You don't mention any names, and I can see that's a good idea, but I just want to hear you tell me that you've told the truth in the story, that you haven't made anything up."

"It's the truth. And you'd be surprised who I'm talking about. But I'll never tell."

"You do an excellent job of conveying the emptiness of these kids' lives," she continued. "Excellent work."

I had finally gotten an unqualified rave from the woman, and I didn't care. Instead, I felt tremendously sad.

"But one other thing," she said. "We need a feature on Homecoming for next Friday's paper—the king and queen, the dance. So make sure you plan to cover it this Friday and follow up by Monday."

My heart began to race; I couldn't write a story on Homecoming if I was taking Sue. That could ruin our date.

"Well, but—"

"Allan, this is an assignment," she said.

"But—"

"Is there a problem?"

I decided to tell a small, white lie. "I don't have a date," I admitted. "I don't want to go without a date."

The Comp looked at me as only the Comp could. "Not having a date isn't the end of the world," she said. Only she could make it sound like a death sentence. "I heard Vicky say that she's going to be there. And she just broke up with her boyfriend. Maybe you two could go together."

I tried to smile and wondered how I would tell Sue.

She was sitting alone in the Spanish classroom when I walked in.

"Did you do the homework?" she asked immediately.

"Yeah," I said, but that wasn't what I wanted to talk about.

"What about exercise four? Did you have any problems with that? I'm lousy with the subjunctive."

"Just a minute," I said. "I have it here. But what about Friday night? Homecoming?"

She wouldn't look up from her book.

"You said you'd see if you could go." I prompted. "With me."

She flapped her hand in front of her face as if she was swatting an imaginary gnat. "Oh, that!" she said. "I can't go with you. I'm going with someone else." I stared at her so long that she added, "Harry Snyder. That's who I'm going with."

Then she grabbed hold of my book and looked at the exercise question.

"What about number three?" she asked.

I took a look, but my heart wasn't in it. I had ruined Sandy's life, now Sue had ruined mine, for the second time.

Chapter Twenty-One

"Did you see the corsage I got Patti?" Rich asked me during dinner Friday night.

Corsages and dates were the last thing I wanted to talk about.

I nodded, then changed the subject. "Where are you guys going tonight?" I asked my parents, while we ate a fast hamburger.

"Party at the Jensens'," my mother said, referring to the owner of one of my father's biggest accounts. "The O'Briens are picking us up."

"I thought you couldn't stand them," I said.

My father looked at me like I was dense. "You don't always do things you like to do," he explained. "Sometimes you do them for business."

"Anyway, they're not so bad," my mother countered.

I tried to look at Homecoming as a boring business deal. I hid out in the press box during halftime. From there, I watched the halftime festivities. The Homecoming candidates were chauffeured around the field in borrowed convertibles, closely followed by the parade of floats. The *Observer*'s float—actually, a bus—brought up the rear.

A two-by-four had been attached to the top of the bus, so that it extended over the hood. A rope was tied to the board and an effigy, approximating a member of the Sundowners, hung from the rope. As the bus ambled onto the track, the dummy was pushed against the front of the bus. Every few feet, Mr Fildew, the head driver, would slam on the brakes, forcing the dummy to fly forward, then smash back against the hood. The flowers Vicky and I had made gaily outlined each window.

After the game, I fled to the locker room to write my story. I kept feeling as if I were in the middle of a bad dream, and no matter how hard I wanted to wake up and have everything be all right, nothing would ever be all right again.

At the dance I headed for the bleachers, far removed from the crowd. Just because I had to cover the dance didn't mean that I had to mingle. And after the king and queen and their court were announced, I could leave.

From the top row of the bleachers I looked down on everyone. The music had started; lots of couples were dancing. Sue and Harry. Vicky and her date, Bob Beekman. I wondered if my story had anything to do with Vicky and Brian's problems. The only person I didn't see was Sandy—she was the person who deserved to be there the most. I had ruined everything. Even Louie Howard was in the far corner of the gym, watching everyone dance. I couldn't help but feel sorry for him.

Just then, I noticed two police officers were standing at the door surveying the crowd. Something was up, and I had to find out what. I stood up and made my way down the bleachers. I walked past the cops and headed for the main door.

"What're the cops doing here?" I asked Eric Pasquale, who was taking tickets. He knew I was covering the dance. "Was there a fight or something?"

"I heard them talking to Mr. Rucker. They're looking for someone," he said. "Some kid. I didn't hear who. I heard them say that they have a warrant for his arrest."

The cops had moved into the gym by the time I got back. I settled back and watched the floor of dancers below me. From time to time I noticed Vicky dancing with Bob. But as I glanced at them again, I saw Brian standing there beside her; Bob was gone. The music was too loud, and I was too far away, but their gestures told the whole story. Brian's arms were pleading for another chance. His legs seemed unsteady. He tried to grab her elbow and lead her farther onto the dance floor. But Vicky held her ground. She wasn't talking, she wasn't responding, she was trying to ignore him. I could see the hurt all over Brian's face, but Vicky was like a statue. I didn't know how the scene was going to work out, but I couldn't stand watching it anymore. I got up and headed for the rest room.

Except for Louie Howard, it was empty when I walked in. Louie was standing at one of the sinks, washing his hands. I wanted time to think, so I chose the closest stall. I had only been there a moment, when the rest room door burst open. Through the crack, I watched Louie Howard drying his hands.

"Hi, Louie," the door crasher called.

I knew the voice anywhere. Brian Sawyer walked past my stall toward Louie.

"Show me your toes," he continued. "I bet you've got some fancy socks on tonight."

It was the typical routine. Brian was holding up six fingers, begging Louie to remove his shoes and socks.

"Show me your toes," he repeated. "I dare you."

Louie was laughing, wanting to take the dare, but he was a little shy. Brian begged some more. Finally, always eager to please, Louie capitulated, and off came one shoe. I wished that, for once, Louie could have learned to say no.

"I'll take that," Brian said, grabbing the shoe.

"Hey, that's mine," Louie said.

"You want it?" Brian asked. "I'll give it to you."

But he held the sneaker over Louie's head, dangling by the shoelaces, just out of his reach. Louie was a little guy, and no matter how high he jumped, he was much too short to even come close. He was laughing and having a good time, even though he should have been mad.

Normally, that would have been the end of the joke. Brian might throw a shoe in the garbage can or hang it from a clock.

But this time Brian was too angry. I couldn't see what he did next, but I heard the flick of his butane lighter. I moved slightly to get a look.

Brian had stuffed a cigarette in his mouth, but instead of lighting it, he was holding the flame under the sneaker. Louie wailed.

I didn't know what to do. If I stayed hidden, Louie's shoe might get burnt. If I intervened, I might get punched out.

"Bri-an, Bri-an," Louie was pleading. Frantically, he was batting at the shoe and the lighter.

"You don't think I'm going to burn up your shoe, do you?" Brian asked.

I swung the stall door open, still buckling my belt.

Startled, Brian jerked his head in my direction.

"Leave him alone," I ordered.

I don't know exactly how it happened. But, whether by accident or defiance, Brian moved his hand that held the lighter. The sneaker burst into flames; Louie screamed.

Brian was standing near a trash can. Without thinking, he threw the shoe toward the open can, filled with paper towels. For a second, nothing happened; the three of us stood there in amazement. Then a wisp of smoke trailed up, finally flames. Brian and Louie looked stunned. I wasn't sure what to do either, but I ripped off my shirt and undershirt, drenched them in the sink, and tried to smother the flames. As the pungent odor of burning rubber filled the room, my shirts went up in flames.

"Get something!" I yelled to Brian, but he wasn't about to help. In a flash, he must have realized what he had done, and he ran out. As he opened the door, Harry was on his way in. A gust of smoke hit him in the face.

"Pull the alarm and get an extinguisher!" I yelled to Harry, as Brian pushed past. Harry darted down the hall.

"Come on, Louie," I said, pushing him toward the door. "Stay here," I said when we were safely in the hall.

"I'll put it out," Harry yelled, as he ran back toward the rest room with a fire extinguisher. The alarm was blaring now, and students were looking around as if someone had played a prank.

"Fire!" I yelled toward the ticket booth. "Get everyone out—there's a fire."

But I didn't have time to help. I was on my way outside. I wasn't going to let Brian get away.

I didn't see him at first. In fact, I didn't see him at all. But I did spot his Camaro in the front row of the parking lot, taking up a handicapped space. As Brian jammed his car into reverse, I saw the white backup lights come on, and I knew he was making his getaway. There was nothing I could do about it, unless I wanted to get run down.

But then I noticed a car driving down the row between Brian's car and the gym. Brian was too agitated to pay any attention. As he stepped on the gas, squealing out of his parking space, he smashed into the passing car. Its hood sprung open, and its radiator spewed water into the air.

It was only then that I recognized the car. Rich had stolen my car again. Brian had nailed him.

TEENAGE CROOKS FOIL EACH OTHER
Burning Sneaker Leads to Smashing Finale

Chapter Twenty-Two

The policemen who had been in the gym handled everything. Within seconds, they were at the scene of the collision.

"Officer, the guy in the Camaro started the fire."

"Did you see it happen?"

"Yes. I was in the bathroom. In a stall, I mean. I was watching what happened. It was kind of an accident, I think," I explained. "I don't think he meant to set it on fire. The other kid—the one in that car—is my brother."

The cop looked at me then and said, "Well, you certainly get around, don't you?" Then he added, "Is there any particular reason you're running around without a shirt? It's forty-five degrees out here."

It was only then that I realized I was shirtless in front of everyone who had come to the dance.

By the time the excitement was over, four fire trucks had roared up. Both Brian and Rich were taken into custody. I thought about calling my parents, but I knew the Jensens had an unlisted phone number, and anyway, I figured they'd rather hear the news personally from Rich.

By the time Brian and Rich had been carted off to the closest police station, the reporters had begun to arrive. We were all standing outside the gym waiting to hear whether we'd get back in. I was certain the dance wouldn't be canceled, since the king and queen hadn't made their entrance yet.

That's when I spotted Harry talking to a reporter from the *Register*.

I made it a point to get close enough to listen.

"You put it out by yourself?" the reporter was asking.

"Yeah," Harry said, as articulate as ever.

"It must've been a pretty big fire by then. Weren't you worried?"

"Not really. It wasn't that big," he said.

Then he spotted me.

"Actually," he continued, "Allan—there—" The reporter turned to look at me. "—told me what to do. He was in the bathroom."

"Allan, what's your last name?" the reporter asked, motioning me to join them.

"Antottle," I said, then spelled it out so he would get it correctly. "I'm a teen correspondent for the *Register*."

The reporter asked me a hundred questions. I knew just what to say.

"What happened to your shirt?" he asked.

"I tried to put it out with my shirt right away, but it practically burst into flames," I said. I watched the reporter write my statement down verbatim.

I was almost done with my interview, when Sue saw us and walked over.

"I've been looking for you everywhere," she said to Harry.

I wondered if Harry had forgotten her. "I put out the fire," Harry told her.

"I thought you left me," she told him.

"Okay," the reporter interrupted. "I see my photographer over there. I want to get your picture."

"But—" I crossed my arms and tried to hide my chest.

A moment later, the photographer appeared.

"You on the right," he said to me, "put your arms down."

"This is just going to be a head shot, right?" I asked.

Then he snapped our photo. Harry and I were standing next to each other. Sue was just behind us, standing in the middle. The reporter went over our names again, asked Sue for hers, then left.

Before I knew it, Harry was shaking my hand.

"Thanks a lot, Allan. You really saved the day," he said.

"But you put the fire out," I said.

"You told me what to do. I'm not sure I would've thought that fast."

"Can't we go in yet?" Sue asked, almost whining. "I'm cold."

"Let's forget the dance," Harry said. "You want to go somewhere and celebrate?"

I thought Harry was asking Sue, then I realized he was talking to me.

"Well, uh—"

"What about the dance?" Sue asked.

"I don't care," Harry said.

"What about me?" she asked.

"You can come, too," he said. "What do you say, Allan?"

"Sure," I said, suddenly realizing Harry wasn't so bad after all. "Let's go to Bob's." Then I was aware that I was shivering. "But I need to get a shirt."

"I don't want to go anywhere but the dance," Sue whined.

"Okay," Harry said and started walking with me toward the parking lot.

"You guys are weird," she said.

For a change, I didn't care.

I didn't get home until after midnight. It was only when I went in the house and discovered that my parents and Rich weren't home that I knew they must have gone to pick him up at the police station. I went to bed.

In the morning, Rich was still in bed when I walked into the kitchen. Both my mother and the Duke were there.

"Exactly what happened last night?" the Duke wanted to know.

"What do you mean?"

"Well, we know what happened with Rich. He won't be leaving the house for quite a long time. But what happened to you?"

Then he slid the *Register* toward me. I looked at the front page:

FAST-THINKING TEENS
STOP OCOTILLO BLAZE

The story was brief and did not mention Brian or Louie by name or the incident in the rest room. The reporter indicated that the fire may have been begun accidentally, but a full investigation was underway.

The picture of us was both a relief and yet more troubling. Harry and I looked a little washed out because of the flash the photographer used, but my chest resembled Tarzan's. Sue looked beautiful, as always. But, for some reason, she was looking right at me with this intense expression. The caption writer must have gotten mixed up and the proofreader must have been on vacation because the caption read:

TEEN HEROES: Harry Snyder (left) and Allen Antottle (right) worked together to put out the fire in Ocotillo High School's gym last night. Allen's date, Sue Arnold, proudly looks on.

My first thought wasn't about Sue or what she would think. I had had enough of her. My first thought was about Sandy: what would she think? I didn't want her to think that I had taken Sue to the dance.

"So what happened?" the Duke asked again.

But as I started to tell him, I couldn't take my mind off Sandy. I had to make things right with her.

And I had to do it today.

Chapter Twenty-Three

A little later that morning, I tried to call Sandy.

"Hello?"

I couldn't miss that cute, sexy voice of hers.

"Hi. How are you?"

She was silent.

"Did you hear about the fire?" I asked, trying to start the conversation.

"I can't talk," she said. "Bye."

"Sandy—"

She had hung up.

I called her again.

"Don't hang up," I said.

"You can't stop me. And we don't have anything to say. I think you said everything."

"But, I just want to—"

"Don't call me again," she said.

Then she hung up the phone.

I spent the day writing my Homecoming story and planning a surprise for Sandy. I wasn't going to take no for an answer.

"I was wondering," I told the Duke awhile after dinner, "if you'd mind if I borrowed the car for an hour or so. I need to see a friend. It's pretty important."

"What about? You're not in trouble, are you?"

"No. I won't be long. I mean, I'll use the bike if you think I shouldn't use the car."

"Go ahead," he said. "Just don't be too late."

"Oh, I won't. Thanks."

Being agreeable had its rewards.

I jumped into the car and made a quick stop before I reached my final destination, Sandy's house. I hid my left hand behind my back and aimed my shaking right hand at the doorbell. I gritted my teeth and waited for someone to answer.

But Sandy almost left me speechless when she opened the door.

"What do you want?" she asked. "I told you not to bother me."

"You said not to call," I corrected her. "So I thought I'd come over in person."

"I don't care if you sent me a telegram, I don't want to see or hear from you." I thought she would slam the door in my face, but she didn't. So I started talking fast.

"I'm from Speedy Delivery Service, and I have something that should have been delivered last weekend."

"What?" She sounded more annoyed than ever.

"Will you sign for it, ma'am?" I asked. My left hand then appeared, holding a hot-fudge sundae from Dairy Queen.

But she wouldn't take it from me. "What're you trying to do, Allan?"

"I'm trying to talk to you. I have my car—can we go somewhere?"

"I don't think we have much to say to each other."

"Then I'd really like it if you'd let me talk to you. Please?"

She stared at me for a while, then she relented. "Maybe for a few minutes. Let me tell my parents."

She was gone for what seemed like forever, while I waited shivering on her front porch, holding the sundae.

"Where're we going?" she asked, when she reappeared in her jacket.

"Some place close. How about Indian Plaza? Okay? That's just around the corner."

"I still don't see why," she said, her voice sounding more distant all the time.

As we walked to the car, I said, "I bought this for you, you know," and offered her the sundae again.

"I don't want it," she told me.

"I don't care if you want it, but—"

"But you can't drive holding it, can you?"

"You were always so perceptive," I said.

"Don't get funny," she replied. "I'm not in the mood."

We reached the plaza in a few minutes, and I parked under a light on the edge of the parking lot, near the dumpsters and away from all of the cars clustered around the mall itself. When I turned the car off, I looked at Sandy, who was holding the sundae as if it were infected.

"Don't be so melodramatic," she told me. "What do you want to say? Just get it over with. I want to go home."

"I'm sorry," I began. "I really am. I shouldn't have done that to you."

"What?" she snapped. "Ask me to the dance? Or gone to Camelback Mountain."

"I shouldn't have asked you to the dance."

"Face it, Allan, you're just embarrassed to be seen with me. That's all there is to it. I didn't know I grossed you out so much."

"How do I know anything?" I asked her. "You kidnapped me. You were all over me in the car. You acted like you were ready to go to bed with me."

She was shocked. "I never meant—"

"Well, that's how you acted," I told her. "But—"

"But what?"

"But you're right in a way. I was worried about what every-one'd think if they saw us together."

"I knew it. I thought you were better than that."

"This is Hairy Allan, remember? I always care what every-body thinks. I thought people would say things about me be-cause I took you out. I know I shouldn't care, but I do. I mean, I don't know if anyone would think anything about it, but if I think they might think it, everything's ruined right there."

"Right, Allan," she said, laughing derisively. "That really makes sense."

"You know what I mean. I just want to be friends. We have been up to this week. Why can't we still be friends?"

"If you can have your problems, I can have mine," she said. "Anyway, you have Sue to be your friend."

"I knew it. I knew you'd get the wrong idea. She's not my friend, and she wasn't my date last night, no matter what the paper said. She was with Harry Snyder. The reporter made a mistake."

"Can I go home now?" she asked. "I'm cold."

"I can turn the heater on," I told her. I started the engine and set the heater on high. "Okay? I just want to know why you can't be friends."

"All right," she said, stirring the melted ice cream and syrup together. "I know I was throwing myself at you." She laughed to herself. "Maybe I shouldn't have done it."

"We're both pretty crazy," I said. "When we want some-thing, we really want it. Only things can get scr—oh, no—"

"What? What's wrong?"

"I popped a contact. I can't believe it. That's never hap-pened before. It just popped out. Don't move."

"Do you want me to help?" she asked.

"No, let me look. It could be anywhere." I made sure it wasn't in the folds of my jeans or my jacket or on the seat near me.

"It wouldn't be on the floor, would it?" she asked.

"God, I hope not."

"Maybe it's on me," she said.

"Don't move, I'll check." I hunched toward her then, trying not to move much, and huddled over her coat, looking for the glint of the lens. I was thinking I should turn on the inside light, when a light suddenly blinded me. I turned my head slowly and saw a police cruiser shining a searchlight at us. Then the cop got out of his car and walked over.

"I don't believe this," Sandy said.

I rolled my window down slowly, still afraid to move and lose my contact forever.

"Do you kids have a problem?"

"No," I told him. "We're just talking."

"I'd go talk some place else," the officer said. "Do you have your license?"

"Do you have a flashlight I could borrow first?" I asked him. "I just lost my contact lens and I'm afraid if I move, I'll break it."

He sighed, but he brought me the flashlight. Then he went back to his cruiser and called in a check on my license plate, while I scoured the car. I had just about given up, when I decided to check my clothes once more. That's when I found the lens, sitting right on the shoulder of my jacket.

By then, the cop had come back and we went through the formalities. He kindly explained the laws on loitering to us. Finally, he told me, "Allan, why don't you take your girl some place nicer than this? You'd enjoy yourselves more, and you wouldn't be liable to get caught in a delicate situation, if you know what I mean."

With that, he left. As soon as I had rolled my window up, Sandy and I burst out laughing.

"Quick, where are we going to go?" I asked. "I better get us out of here."

"Why don't you drive to the Dairy Queen and let's get a replacement," she said. "This is like soup. For a moment, I thought I was going to have to eat it all to look for your contact."

The car was beginning to warm up now, as I pulled out of the lot.

"I think we deserve another chance," I told her, seizing the opportunity. "I mean, we don't have to go out on a date right away. It probably wouldn't be a good idea. We don't have to do things in such a rush."

"Right," she said, smiling at me. "Let's start with a hot-fudge sundae and work our way up to dessert."

* * * * *

Miss Stapleton, our English teacher, had given us the hour to write something about ourselves. Goals. Loves. Poignant moments. Relationships. Things high-school juniors are supposed to know about. Miss Stapleton's life is obviously boring, so she gets her kicks reading about ours.

Actually, I really like Stapleton. The first time the class wrote themes to hand in, she told me I was a sensitive, intelligent, artistic person with a great potential. You can't dislike someone who tells you stuff like that.

Potential? I wonder. Parents divorced. Mom hanging around with a creep. At the same time, she's at me every minute to do something with my life.

Meet Natalie Draper. In addition to all of the above, she's got a boyfriend named Don and a new best buddy named Cozy. Want to hear the whole story? Read

MAYONNAISE ON FRENCH FRIES
by Bette Ward Widney.
Available from Crosswinds in November.

How do you break up with a sweet guy like Ernie?
As Amy soon finds out,

IT ISN'T EASY!

For a good laugh, read

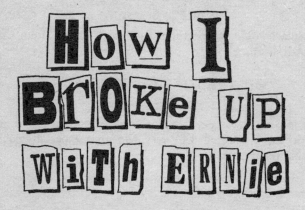

HOW I
BROKe UP
WiTh ERNie

by R.L. Stine

Available from Crosswinds in September

COMING NEXT MONTH
FROM
CROSSWINDS™

BUMMER SUMMER
by Phyllis Green

Stuart would do just about anything to get to Mountain Adventure.

HOW I BROKE UP WITH ERNIE
by R.L. Stine

Breaking up is hard to do, especially when it's with Ernie. How would Amy ever manage it, especially now that she'd met Colin?

AVAILABLE THIS MONTH

THE HOUSE WITH THE IRON DOOR
Margaret Mary Jensen

FROG EYES LOVES PIG
James Deem

Blushing Beauty—Do's and Don'ts

Avoid colors that are very different from your natural cheek color.

A defined line looks unnatural. Blend your rouge well so no one can see where color begins or ends.

Don't blush in a strip so wide that it covers your entire face. Blush is used to highlight cheekbones and add color to the face. Don't overdo.

Never apply blusher too close to the center of your face. Feel your face. Notice that the prominent part of your cheekbone starts around the area under the center of your eye, not at the bridge of your nose.

Practice with gels. A little squirt goes a long way.

Applying blush without a mirror is a mistake. Always watch what you're doing.

Don't apply blush before foundation. If you're wearing foundation, apply it first, blush second.

If you've tried applying a little blush as directed above but feel that you'd like to make a little more (or less) of your face shape, there are a few contouring tricks you can try with cheek color. Be sure to play and practice at home to see what works best for you. A few afternoons in front of the mirror will make you a makeup pro!

1. Think about the shape of your face. Is it square? Round? Rectangular? Triangular? Oval?

2. A hint for the round face: Put a dot of color on your chin and blend it in. This will help lengthen your face a bit.

3. Is your face long and narrow, like a rectangle? To soften the hard lines and widen your face, concentrate blush on the outer edges of your face. This will draw attention away from the length and give more width where you need it.

4. To minimize the hard lines of a square face, apply blusher normally, then dot a bit of extra color on your chin and the middle of your forehead. Blend well.

5. Triangular or heart-shaped face? Avoid putting blusher on your chin. It will only call attention to it.

6. Oval face? Anything goes. Try a hint of blush on earlobes, too, to give a fresh, country look—as if you've just come in from the great outdoors.